Monarch Mystery

A Butterfly Researcher's Journal

Book design by Jake Slavik
Illustrations by Arpad Olbey

Design Elements: Shutterstock Images

Published in the United States by Jolly Fish Press, an imprint of North Star Editions, Inc.

First Edition
First Printing, 2018

Library of Congress Cataloging-in-Publication Data (pending)
978-1-63163-184-9 (paperback)
978-1-63163-183-2 (hardcover)

Jolly Fish Press
North Star Editions, Inc.
2297 Waters Drive
Mendota Heights, MN 55120
www.jollyfishpress.com

Printed in the United States of America

Monarch Mystery

A Butterfly Researcher's Journal

by J. A. Watson

Illustrations by Arpad Olbey | Text by Amanda Humann

JOLLY
FiSH
PRESS
Mendota Heights, Minnesota

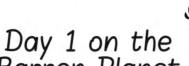

Day 1 on the Barren Planet

Pick Your Own Path:

You have arrived on the barren planet, where the food, weather, and local inhabitants are completely bizarre. You:

A. Panic, steal a spaceship, and head for home. Turn to page 98. Page 98: You're caught by the Pig People of Pluto, and you live out your life in their zoo, begging for Piggy McJiggles Snax for Humans from zoo visitors.

B. Embrace it and try to blend in. Turn to page 57. Page 57: You blend in too well and become part of the hive mind, like an ant—which is fine until invaders from Mars invent a giant magnifying glass and use it with the sun's rays to burn your planet.

C. Suck it up and try not to whine. Turn to page 66. Page 66: You are rewarded with a fuzzy, mild-mannered creature with eight legs who will become your new sidekick.

So far, my new spider is the only good thing about moving to Dallas. Mom gave her to me as my "not whining in front of Izzy about moving" bribe. Who knew a little sister could come in so handy? I must have been great at faking the enthusiasm. I could have ended up with a millipede or some other boring insect like a butterfly instead of an arachnid. But my tarantula is AWESOME.

What isn't awesome is Texas. It's flat and brown like the alien planets in classic *Star Trek* episodes. The only difference is that the people don't have lizard heads or speak in hisses. It's too bad they don't. It would be hilarious to see kids at the mall eating ice cream cones with forked tongues and claws! Maybe it would look something like this:

Back home, Belle Lake wasn't a huge city like Dallas. But at least it had hills, and you could see mountains and smell ocean air. And, like pretty much all of western Washington, it was covered in green. I miss looking in all that green for garter snakes with Jack and Dawson. We didn't have any venomous snakes in Belle Lake. Guess how many Dallas has? FOUR SPECIES. I looked them up online before we moved.

I know Mom's excited to live in an area with a larger population of people with Mexican heritage like us, but she could have been an accounting manager anywhere. We could have moved to somewhere cool like California, but *noooo*, she got a job in *Texas*. It's weird here, even without the lizard heads. The people talk weird, it smells weird, and the weather is weird—it's still sunny enough here to wear shorts and flip-flops even though school starts in less than a week! WEIRD.

And speaking of school, I'm even more worried than I was before the move. Just writing about it makes my stomach gurgle. I realized today that I've known all my friends pretty much all my life. I've never had to make new ones. Is making friends like riding a bicycle? Will I remember how it works? What if I don't?

On the one hand, Brenton Park will be a whole school full of smart people, since it's a magnet school for kids interested in science. And that should make it easier, since I *know* science. Highest grades in class + always the leader for our projects in school + speaker for our Science Squad = science guy extraordinaire, right?

But on the other hand, writing pick-your-own-path stories and loving science fiction might make me look like I don't belong there. I guess I'll just have to act like I know what I'm doing and pretend to be Mr. Awesome Knower of All Things, Especially Things about Spiders.

I wonder if you could walk a spider? Like put a tiny harness and leash on her somehow? Then I could take her outside and scare that pinched-up old lady who lives on the other side of our duplex. The face she made when the movers unloaded my bug-net-launcher project looked like she was smelling week-old gym socks stuffed with cooked cabbage. Wait 'til she sees my tarantula!

Which reminds me: I think I will name my tarantula Worf, like the Klingon in *Star Trek: The Next Generation*. There was that one episode where the actor playing Worf gets red paint on his knees, and then in the next scene, it's gone. I know my new pet is a girl, but she's a Mexican red-knee tarantula. Get it? *Red knee*?

Technically, the term Mexican red-knee is used to refer to a couple different species of tarantulas. To be specific, scientists would use the Latin name *Brachypelma hamorii*, or *B. hamorii*, to identify Worf. The other species that sometimes gets called a Mexican red-knee is *B. smithi*. These spiders look similar to *B. hamorii*, but they're actually two different kinds of spiders!

B. smithi and *B. hamorii* look and act the same to me. And all tarantulas have the same mellow temperament, and that's what I really care about. The only reason I even know Worf is a *B. hamorii* is because the breeder labeled her cage.

Oh, there goes my stomach again. Maybe it's just noisy because it's lunchtime.

And speaking of lunch, maybe I should feed ~~my new tarantula~~ Worf. She's probably really hungry after getting acclimated to her new home in my room. I bet she feels like she's landed on an alien planet too. Maybe I'll put a model of the *Starship Enterprise* next to her cage to make her feel safe.

Day 8 on the Barren Planet

I've spent pretty much the whole time since we got here unpacking and going shopping for school with Mom and Izzy. This is the first chance I've had in the last couple of days to catch up on this journal—and just in time for the first day of school!

So far, Brenton Park is just like any other school, except that there are more kids wearing shirts that say funny, smart things like "Oh no, 7 ate 9!" and "Will code for candy." And there are some cowboy boots, although not nearly as many as I thought there would be. The halls are boring and plain except for some bright posters advertising a Day of the Dead Festival. That's kind of cool—we didn't have a festival for Day of the Dead back home.

I hoped I didn't stick out as the new kid, since all the other sixth graders are new too. They're starting over like me, since they're from all over the school district. We all looked sort of lost. It made me feel better, even though I still missed my friends. So I decided to start SOMNF (Special Operation Make New Friends).

I couldn't wait for science class, because I was pretty sure that was where I'd finally find someone to hang out with. I have science right after lunch, so as soon as the bell rang signaling the end of lunch, I sprinted down the hall to my science classroom. The doors opened, and I was greeted by the familiar sight of black-topped lab tables and that weird moist smell from something wet living in a tank in the back of the room. It felt like home.

Mr. Eagon, the sixth-grade science teacher, is ~~way better than my old science teach~~ awesome. He's thin, wiry, and super funny. Turns out Mr. Eagon is also in charge of the Brenton Park Science Squad! He said there'd be a short Squad sign-up meeting right after school. He also said we could take turns bringing in our own pets to show everyone during our life science unit. I ran to sign up Worf for the first slot. She's sure to impress someone.

Then Mr. Eagon went over safety rules and stuff like that. While he did that, I got a good look around. I saw lots of beakers and flasks, some posters on the walls of various animal life cycles, and a locked cabinet that I hope is full of stuff that blows up. I saw that there's also a separate storage/lab room through a door on one end marked with a sign that says "Science Squad Lab."

I scouted around for ~~possible friends~~ SOMNF. I spotted one kid who has to be the blandest human I've ever seen. Everything about him was khaki: his hair, his T-shirt, his pants. I couldn't see his socks, but I'll bet they were khaki too. It was sort of creepy. I probably wouldn't even have noticed him, except he was writing in a journal. Maybe he's a writer too. *SOMNF target acquired!*

I suffered through a study period and band before I got to go back to my science class for the Squad meeting.

The classroom filled up with lots of kids from sixth through eighth grade. We all wrote our names on a list as we came in. There were so many of us, they had to add a second sheet of paper. Mr. Eagon and two other teachers talked in the corner for what seemed like forever. Then they announced that we had so many sign-ups that each grade would get their own Squad and project, which was exciting, but even better was that sixth grade got Mr. Eagon!

As the older kids shuffled out, I looked around the room to see who was left. There was a girl wearing coveralls, like mechanics wear, sitting next to me. Her blond, springy hair was shoved into a greasy baseball hat about two sizes too small. When I say greasy, I mean the hat actually had part of a greasy handprint over the top. Maybe she didn't know it was there. I debated whether to mention it to her.

She waved, and I looked behind me to see the kid in khaki with the journal wave back. The girl smiled at us and said, "Hey, Thurmond! Hey . . . new guy!"

"You guys know each other?" I blurted. Whatever happened to "from all over the school district"?

"Oh yeah, we totally do. I'm Lyla, by the way, and this is Thurmond." She waved a hand at the khaki kid, who gave me a neutral smile. "And that's Caden and Gavin on the other side of the room by the door. We were all on the same Science Squad last year."

"*You all went to school together?*" Dang it! There were only a few other kids in the room besides this group. I *was* the new guy. My confidence shifted a bit.

"Oh no, not at all. None of our schools had enough kids to fill a Squad, so they created a district-wide one. Unfortunately, it looks like I'm the only girl from our Squad who decided to attend Brenton Park." She sighed. I felt bad for her. I also guessed she'd still want to know about the grease stain on her hat, so I told her.

She laughed. "That's just about the nicest thing anyone's said to me today." Then she leaned in closer. "Don't worry," she said, as if confiding in me, "I know all about the handprint. In fact, I left it there on purpose."

"Why?"

She took off her hat and held it tenderly, like a puppy. "Because that right there is the handprint of Mr. Bobby James Torque."

"Who's that? That sounds like one of those race car driver names," I said.

"'*WHO'S THAT*'?!" she screeched, eyes wide. "Bobby James Torque is only about the BEST NASCAR DRIVER EVER!"

I held my hands up. "Okay, okay!"

14

She calmed down immediately. "I went to see a NASCAR race with my daddy when I was only seven, and we got pit passes. I actually met Bobby James Torque. Can you believe it?" She got a dreamy look on her face, like Izzy gets when she sees a candy store. "And he was working with the crew on the car—he's old-fashioned like that—and had grease on his hand, and he patted me on the head to say hi. It was just about the best day of my life."

"You like cars, huh? Cool." A chance to impress! I went for it. "So which do you think is better: horsepower or torque?" I just used the only words I know about cars that seemed science-ish. I thought maybe she'd just be so impressed that I even knew what those things were that she wouldn't register what I'd said. I thought wrong.

She giggled, her eyes crinkling in the corners. "You are SO funny! That's the best joke! Especially since torque and horsepower aren't really in competition. You use torque along with rpm to *calculate* horsepower."

"The new kid's hi-larious!" she said to Thurmond, who gave her a huge smile (but ignored me). She whacked me on the shoulder. "That's great. We could use a comedian!"

Just then, Mr. Eagon called the meeting to order. "Welcome to Science Squad!" he said. "It looks like we have five members this year. That's great! I hope you're all ready for a fantastic year full of discoveries!"

Then he read the Science Squad requirements out loud, explaining that we would be doing actual citizen science work (involving several hours of work outside of school) to help real scientists solve real problems. I think he also said something about doing projects to earn badges, but I wasn't really listening. I had already earned several badges with my old Squad.

But then he said something that caught my attention: "Now, Brenton Park normally sends the Science Squad to the city-level competition, but we have three Squads this year and a budget for only one Squad to go. So you will be competing with the seventh- and eighth-grade Squads for that opportunity. You all get a chance to impress a panel of judges—all science teachers—between now and Thanksgiving break. Then we'll choose the Squad with the best project to represent us. Hope you're all ready for a challenge!"

"Boogity, boogity, boogity! Let's go racin', boys!" said Lyla. The rest of the Squad groaned.

"What?" she said, clearly shocked that no one got her reference. "That's what the announcer yells at the start of NASCAR races. This'll be great! A little competition never hurt anyone. It's the only way to know what you can really do."

"Those Squads have more experience than us," said Thurmond.

"What's the worst that can happen?" asked Lyla. "We lose to a more experienced Squad, and no one's really surprised because the odds were against us. But when a rookie wins against a seasoned driver, he becomes the king of the track and everyone adores him! Don't y'all want to at least try for total adoration?"

I looked around the group. Caden and Gavin (I still don't actually know which one is which) still looked a little nervous, but Thurmond never took his eyes off Lyla as he smiled wide and nodded.

"That's the spirit, everyone!" said Mr. Eagon. "All Squads will be doing active citizen science, helping to work on a real research project. This year, the eighth graders will be focusing on chemistry, the seventh graders are focusing on robotics, and you are focusing on biology." He glanced at the clock. "Here's a list of possible projects, although I'm open to suggestions. We've run out of time today, so we'll discuss it and take a vote at our next meeting."

We didn't really get a chance to talk because everyone took their lists and sprinted out of the room (or at least it seemed like it), but maybe I can wow the Squad with all my scientific knowledge at our next meeting.

Special ~~Ops~~ OOPS

Today we met for our first official Science Squad meeting. This was supposed to be my chance to put SOMNF into motion. I was really excited to get to know everyone and maybe see if I could ask Thurmond about his writing. But that isn't even close to what happened.

Mr. Eagon was out sick today, so we had a sub for class. She led the Science Squad meeting too, so we saved the voting for our project for when Mr. Eagon was back. This time, we just did introductions. The sub asked each of us to say what our favorite science-related subjects were. We started with Lyla.

"Hi, I'm Lyla, and I'm just real excited to be here. I love mechanical things and engines and how they work, especially in race cars for NASCAR." Everyone nodded except Thurmond, who was busy writing in his journal.

I went next. I'd practiced a funny-but-smart introduction in my head, so I launched right into it. "Hi," I said, "I'm Humberto Smythe-Lopez, but you guys can call me Bertie. I like zoological sciences, and I'm especially interested in spiders. I'm not from Texas, but I was on a really amazing Science Squad in my old school." Pretending to be confident, I went on, "I was kind of the leader, like I was the speaker when we did presentations, and I know I can totally be a great leader here too."

Then I threw in some good stuff—the humor punch: "Or I will be, if I can learn to talk like a Texan and maybe do a few other weird things like choke down barbecue all the time, solve the mystery of why people here like football so much, and find ways to avoid the freaky weather. I'd rather be watching *Star Trek* or playing *Space Jelly Hunters*, am I right?" These were my fellow nerds, so I figured they weren't into what must be Texas clichés. I gave a little laugh and looked around. Lyla laughed with me, but no one else did.

In fact, it went dead silent in the room, and the other members of the Squad were all glaring at me. The silence stretched out. You could hear a spider drop from the ceiling it was so quiet.

The sub cleared her throat and asked Caden to go next. Caden is skinny, and his hair sticks straight up.

He said, "I'm Caden Wu, and I really love barbecue. My family and I *compete* in barbecue competitions around the country, and we've won first place in the Dallas Pig and Pitmaster Cook-Off three years in a row now. I like food science, and I'm particularly interested in the Maillard reaction. You know, when something sweet can get nice and crusty?"

Then he stared right at me and said, "Because it's not good when things get *salty*."

I cringed. I hadn't meant to insult him. Maybe that was why everyone except for Lyla looked so mad.

I was going to apologize, but then Thurmond (dressed all in khaki again today) spoke up. I crossed my fingers that he wasn't a barbecue fan too.

He said, "I'm Thurmond, and I *love* football because sports physics is the best part of science. How could someone not love football? *Everybody* loves football— at least everybody with a brain." He frowned in my direction. "As my favorite quote says, 'The devil is in the details,' and football is full of fascinating details. It has it all: vectors, biomechanics, and stats. And speaking of stats, did you know that I have an IQ of 168? So I don't think we'll be needing a leader."

I shrank down into my chair. I opened my mouth again, but Gavin, the last Squad member, cut me off. He wore a huge watch that swallowed his wrist, and he spoke really fast. "I'm Gavin, and I'm not into barbecue or football." I gave him a weak smile. If he didn't care about those things, then why did he glare too? He continued, "But I'm really into our 'freaky weather.' My two oldest brothers are storm chasers. They say I'm too young to come along, but as soon as I'm old enough, I'll be right out there with them."

I'd insulted everyone but Lyla without even trying. I tried not to look directly at anyone. I didn't think I could take any more glaring.

I felt so stupid. I was trying to figure out what to say to retract it all, working it over in my head, but I couldn't figure out how to fix it.

I was relieved when the sub let us go early.

Missing Home

~~I can't wait to tell J~~

I keep forgetting I can't just go next door and tell Jack things—like about Science Squad or the guy I saw at the grocery store the other day. He was a dead ringer for the alien boss at the end of level 51 in *Space Jelly Hunters*, except he was wearing a cowboy hat. I guess I could chat with Jack on the computer, but it isn't the same. We can't send secret coded messages just by hanging our socks in our windows for each other to see across the alley.

Here's the code so I never forget:

- One sock: come over.
- Two socks: sleepover in the tent outside!
- One dirty sock: stuck doing homework.
- Two dirty socks: chores and forced family time.

Maybe I could use a modified sock code on the neighbor lady, because I'm pretty sure she's not friend material:

- *One dirty sock: stop frowning.*
- *Two dirty socks: really, stop frowning—your face might get stuck like that.*

Oh well. I promise I will never talk about home again. It shall henceforth be known as The Place Not Named.

I'm now sitting here in my room with Worf, my only friend. I told her about my day. She's a good listener, but she doesn't seem to have any advice to give. More spider stuff and Texas weirdness to come.

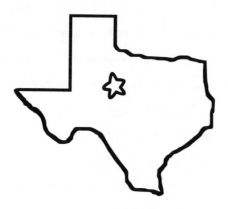

Good News and Bad News

The good news is that I realized today that Worf might not be my only friend. I guess I'm sort of friends with Lyla too. Which isn't so bad, since she thinks I'm funny. It's kind of weird since she's the only girl, but she has my back, like in the Squad meeting this afternoon when we picked our project.

The project is the bad news.

Mr. Eagon said it might be a good idea to stick to something with relevance to our local lives to make it more important to everyone. So we started naming science things that are local, but Mr. Eagon said no to all of them. His reasons varied from "I'm not sure there's a citizen science project related to torque in a race car" to "I'm thinking it might be hard on our budget to buy that much pork."

"I have an idea," I said. "I heard someone's trying to repopulate the tarantula population in North Texas

25

near Lewisville. They're letting hundreds of 'slings'—that's short for spiderlings, or baby spiders—loose into the wild to try and save their numbers." I hoped the use of spider slang would get everyone interested.

"What do you see the Squad doing?" asked Mr. Eagon.

"We could learn all sorts of things by raising our own slings to let go here." Inside my head I thought, *And I'll impress everyone by being our spider expert!*

"I think it could be interesting," Lyla said, nodding her head.

"Um, no, spiders are kind of creepy," said Caden, shuddering.

"I have something that would work much better," said Thurmond. "You know how we have monarch butterflies coming through here in fall? We could—"

"Wait, what? Texas gets butterflies in fall?" I asked quickly, not wanting to give up on the tarantula idea so fast. "And what the heck could be scientifically important about a bunch of fancy-pants insects dressed up in pretty colors?"

"Yes, we have monarch butterflies here in fall, BLURTIE," said Thurmond. "And there are plenty of things that we could study about them, including the fact that several of their migration flyways converge through Texas every year. Plus, there are lots of different citizen science projects tied to them."

Everyone nodded. I stayed silent, worried I'd just earned myself a new nickname—one I didn't want to stick.

"Excellent idea, Thurmond," Mr. Eagon said. "Let's take a vote. All in favor of raising tarantulas?"

Only I raised my hand.

"All in favor of studying monarchs?"

Every other hand in the room went up. Thurmond's smug smile was so irritating, I couldn't help it. It just came out: "WHAT?! You don't really want to study butterflies, do you? It's . . . it's . . ." I looked around, and most of the Squad faces were scowling.

Normally, I'd be worried about the fact that a bunch of people looked mad at me, and I'd try to say something to fix it. But I thought I had lost any chance with them already. So I just stopped talking completely for the rest of the meeting.

Lyla smiled at me on the way out, but the other guys were still scowling.

"See you tomorrow, Blurtie," Thurmond said, and Caden and Gavin laughed.

Yep, I can already tell this year's gonna be awful.

Monarch migration is like a relay. In the spring, monarchs begin flying north from Mexico. But they only make part of the journey. Several generations of monarchs keep flying north. In the fall, the monarchs change directions and begin to migrate south. This generation of butterflies lives much longer. A single butterfly may fly thousands of miles from the northern United States and Canada to reach Mexico. These butterflies stay in Mexico during the winter before beginning the journey north again in spring.

Fighting among the Ranks, Part 1

It's a good thing that I have study period right now and nothing to work on, because I don't think I can concentrate anyway. Besides, I wanted to write this down while it's still fresh in my mind.

Lyla sat with me again today at lunch. I was a little worried about what the rest of the Squad might think, but they didn't really pay attention to us—except for Thurmond, who kept frowning and staring at us. Weird.

I wondered why Lyla chose to hang out with me, especially after I made everyone on the Squad mad again. So I swallowed my pride and asked.

She was eating butterscotch pudding. She licked her spoon clean, closed her eyes and sighed, and then put it down.

"Don't take this the wrong way, Bertie, but I felt sorry for you. I thought you were funny, and when you talk to me, you don't seem so . . ."

"Stupid?"

"Big-headed," she said, and I cringed.

"I don't mean to be rude," she said, "but when you're around the rest of the Squad, you get all eager to perform, like a hunting dog trying to prove himself."

Suddenly, a peanut butter and jelly sandwich flew over to us and landed on the table behind Lyla, plopping in a squishy heap between two seventh graders' lunch trays. The two kids shifted to get out of the way, and I recognized them from the Science Squad informational meeting. Then we all turned to see where the sandwich had come from and spotted three eighth graders, also from Science Squad. They were holding a homemade catapult four tables away, and they were waving. The seventh graders scowled back at them, then exchanged glances as they reached under their table.

Lyla and I looked at each other for a second before we realized what soaring sandwiches and reaching under the table meant: We were about to get caught in a war zone.

"Duck and cover!" I yelled, scrunching down. Lots of excited yelling and scrambling happened at the tables between the two opposite sides of the food fight.

"Oh my stars!" said Lyla, sitting straight up in the line of fire. "Really? This is ridiculous! How old—" She stopped talking as a whirring noise started behind her.

The seventh graders had pulled out several small aerial drones and were deploying their air defense. One of the drones came to our table and hovered a bit before dropping down on top of Lyla's pudding and flying away with it.

"Noooo!" yelled Lyla. "Not my butterscotch! My mama's on a low-carb diet, and I only get one of those every two weeks! Dang it!" She turned to me with a very determined look on her face. "I'm going after it."

"Best of luck, hope you make it out alive," I said while I tried to squiggle off the bench and under the table. She bolted away, her eyes locked on her target, dodging as smaller foods were lobbed from both sides. I ~~reached~~

Oops, gotta go, the teacher's coming! I'll tell the rest of the story later!

Fighting among the Ranks, Part 2

Okay, so I'm back at home now and ready to continue . . .

Pick Your Own Path:

War has erupted between two alien planets that use food as weapons, and you are stuck between them. Alien forces have kidnapped your companion's beloved dessert. You:

<u>A</u>. Try to intercept the flying food missiles and lob them back at both sides. Turn to page 86. Page 86: Both sides focus on you instead, and you are buried under a mountain of discarded sandwiches, stale egg rolls, and orange peels. You try to eat your way out, but there's just too much, so you chew a comfy hole into the mountain and live out your days talking to a rotting liverwurst sandwich while you wait to be rescued.

<u>B</u>. Pick a side and fight nobly for them. Turn to page 43. Page 43: Your side wins the war, but your allies

decide that your best use now is as a food source. The aliens grant you one last wish, so you choose to be made into a giant spaceberry pie. The aliens are allergic to spaceberries and die after eating the pie, proving that there are no winners in war.

<u>C</u>. Take the cowardly but safest way out.

I chose C, obviously.

I reached on top of the table and grabbed what remained of my lunch: a tuna fish sandwich. I considered turning it into a tuna fish submarine and flinging it under the tables and onto the lap of the seventh grader piloting a drone. No one thinks to defend themselves down low during an air raid like this. It would have been a great moment in food-fight history, but I was too hungry. I snarfed it down.

Gavin ran past my table yelling, "One hundred percent chance of meatball sub precipitation!" A piece of ground beef fell by his left foot, and another drone whizzed by. I watched legs running past the ends of the tables and food shrapnel splattering in small pools around them. I listened to the tables creaking as kids

jumped onto them for better angles to chuck their chow.
I had to get out of the main action.

Food thudded on the table right above me. I was
about to flee when I realized I'd left my backpack
out on the table, totally wide open and undefended. I
grabbed it and flicked a few remnants of cupcake off of
it, resisting the urge to lick my fingers. I was lucky there
wasn't more food splattered on it.

Shuffling my backpack under the table and onto my
back, I searched for the best place to be in a food fight:
a sturdy table, usually near an exit so you can bolt when
the teachers start grabbing kids.

I saw one by the exit to the courtyard. No one was
sitting there. It was perfect cover. A quick scurry from
table to table, and I finally found a little more peace.
There were two other kids under there, shrinking back
against the wall.

Food still plopped randomly in front of the table,
but not as much as where I'd been sitting. I could hear
the whir of the drones flying around the room and the
screeches as they dumped whatever they were carrying
onto the heads of unsuspecting targets.

"Geez, where are the teachers?" I asked.

One of the kids said, "I'm guessing all the lunch monitors were mysteriously called away to the office, and then Barton Twisp—that big guy over there—found some way to lock the doors from the inside. Every year, someone in the eighth grade starts a food fight in the first week of school, and—uh oh, here comes Barton!"

We scrambled to a safer location as Barton charged toward our table and jumped on top, along with his two lieutenants who were carrying the catapult. Food chunks rained down. There was a crashing noise at the other end of the cafeteria, and the eighth graders leapt from the table and ran back across the room.

That was when I spotted Lyla finally catching up with the drone. She was splattered with ketchup and gravy, but her eyes were clear enough to see the drone hover and start to tip the pudding container. She pushed the intended target out of the way, and he yelled a muffled "Thanks!" as he crawled to safety. Then Lyla flipped over and slid on her back onto the lunch table, opening her mouth wide just as the pudding fell. It landed straight in her mouth!

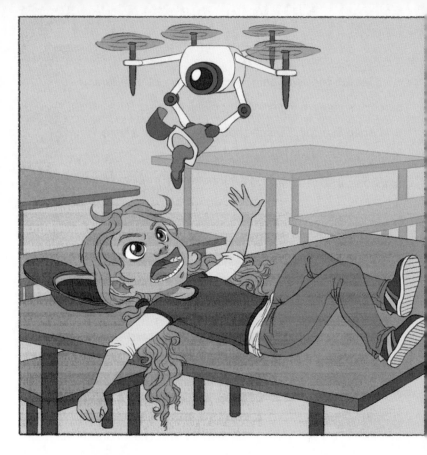

The onlookers went nuts, chanting, "Ly-LA! Ly-LA!" as she hopped to her feet and held up her arms in victory. "Go, Lyla, go!!" I yelled, but I lost sight of her as another volley of food bits started.

When the teachers finally broke in and busted things up, I managed to slip out the exit without being seen. I don't know who won, but that eighth-grade Squad made their point: THE COMPETITION IS ON!

Basic Training

Is it weird that the best day at school so far involved airborne spaghetti? Since the food fight, Lyla's one of the most popular kids at our school. Everyone's heard her butterscotch pudding story, and someone even caught it on video and posted it somewhere. Hanging with her is like being a celebrity buddy.

Our Squad meeting today was full of more butterfly talk. But it's not as bad as I thought. I walked into the room really not getting why anyone cares so much about butterflies. I wanted to ask, but I figured I'd upset everyone again.

Mr. Eagon must read minds. He looked right at me first, then at the group as he said, "You guys picked a great subject for the fall project! But monarch butterflies have a limited life span, and we only have so much of fall left to do this. I'll give you a little info to kick off our project, and then you guys can get started right away. Deal?"

We all nodded. It's not like any of us would say no. Why do teachers always ask that sort of thing when there really isn't any other answer?

"The monarch migration is one of the most amazing things that occurs in nature," said Mr. Eagon. "It's a complete scientific puzzle. We don't know why they travel so far, especially because it takes four or more generations of butterflies before the full round-trip is complete. It's like your great-grandma left Mexico and moved north, then your grandparents were born and moved farther north, and then your parents moved even farther north. Then you were born, and somehow you knew how to switch directions and move all the way back to Mexico for the winter, traveling three thousand miles south to a place you've never been."

That was just like me! My family had lived up north for three generations, and now we'd moved south. That was kind of cool. I imagined my whole family with butterfly wings. I almost laughed out loud when I pictured Great-Auntie Fortuna as a butterfly trying to get nectar from a flower. I managed to wrangle my imagination back just in time to hear about scientific theories.

"Scientists are not sure why monarchs do this," said Mr. Eagon. "Some scientists think the monarchs follow the bloom of milkweed when they move north and then move south when plants die off and winter comes. Others think monarchs move out of areas where there are a lot of butterflies infected with parasites by summer's end. Your research might help them solve this migration mystery."

Mr. Eagon continued, "Doing research on monarchs is also important because butterflies are pollinators. They help plants reproduce, and some of those plants, such as alfalfa and red clover, are the basis of food sources for the livestock we depend on. And I'm sure this is of most importance to you all: Some plants also provide food for humans."

Food. That made me remember that butterflies are also a food source for spiders. I guess saving butterflies might not be all bad.

"I think you can all find something about monarchs that is important to you," Mr. Eagon went on. "Even if it is just for spider food," he said, smiling at me.

See? He's a mind reader. Then he went on: "The numbers of monarchs, however, have been dropping year after year. So your project is to find and tag wild monarch butterflies for a group of scientists in the Monarch Tag and Track project."

"Tag?" said Caden, guffawing. "How the heck do you tag a butterfly? You'd squish it! And who makes radio transmitters that small?"

"These tags don't send out signals," Mr. Eagon explained. "Instead, they label the butterflies. Each tag is a tiny sticker made of plastic. The stickers are flat, round, and very small—just a little wider than a pencil eraser—and they have very small print on them."

"We won't hurt the monarchs or anything if we handle them?" asked Gavin.

"It's okay to handle them, and the older caterpillars too," said Mr. Eagon. "If we find caterpillars or chrysalises, we will collect and raise them for tagging and release too. Now, you may have heard that raising monarchs is controversial," he went on. "It's okay for us as citizen scientists to raise any wild monarchs we find, but it's true that entomologists who study monarchs don't support large-scale commercial raising of monarchs. They are concerned it could put wild monarchs at risk for disease or have an impact on monarch genetics. So it is *very* important that we only catch, tag, and release wild butterflies during this project."

He went on and described how each tag has a unique number on it. Each number is recorded in a database. We'll track data (like where we tagged the monarch and released it) and then enter it into the database for that tag number. If someone else finds that butterfly, they can look up its tag number and add data (like when and where they found it). What's amazing is that some of the tagged butterflies are found months later, thousands of miles from where they were tagged!

No tarantula, to my knowledge, has ever traveled thousands of miles on its own, much less been tagged and released and recaptured that far from the starting point. Score a point for butterflies.

"I'd like you guys to take the lead now and decide what you need to learn about monarchs," Mr. Eagon said. "You'll also need to plan what tasks you need to do to complete this project. You'll have to work fast. Within six weeks or so, the vast majority of these butterflies will have moved south. So the longer you wait, the harder they'll be to find. I'll come back in about an hour to check your progress."

Lyla volunteered to write things down, going to the whiteboard after Mr. Eagon left. I wanted to lead the conversation, but I knew that pushing my luck with this crowd right now wouldn't be smart.

We made a list of the things we needed to know. There was so much to learn that we decided we would each become an expert in one part of monarch knowledge. Then at the next Squad meeting, we'd teach each other the basics of what we needed to know. That way, we'd save time and still have experts in each area. Plus, we might get a sticker added to our Science Squad profiles.

There are a bunch of different kinds of stickers that Science Squad members can earn. So far, I have three:

- **Research:** for my project studying naked mole rats in fourth grade.
- **Education:** for teaching the kindergarteners about earthworms. Good thing I caught that one kid who tried to EAT my specimens!
- **Action:** for spending a semester picking up litter.

These stickers are posted on my profile page on the Science Squad website for everyone to see. Maybe if we teach people about monarchs, I'll get another education sticker!

Anyway, back to the Science Squad meeting . . . I was thinking I'd take the task of researching and teaching the group about the butterfly life cycle and raising caterpillars. Maybe it could come in handy for learning how to raise my own tarantula food. I imagined wearing a chef's hat, leaning over Worf's tank with a silver platter, and showing her the "Bug of the Day."

But Thurmond claimed this topic while I was daydreaming. Gavin said he'd study how and where to find monarchs, and Caden volunteered to be the expert on the feeding and care of captive butterflies.

Lyla turned from the board and said, "I guess I'll teach us about catching, handling, and tagging."

"So, Blurtie," said Thurmond, "that means you get to teach us how to identify monarch butterflies. Let me make your job easy: Tarantulas have eight legs, and monarchs have six legs and wings."

I gave him my best *duh* look.

"Don't put your hard tires on, Thurmond," said Lyla. "We're all gonna do our parts just fine."

We showed Mr. Eagon our plan when he came back, and he seemed impressed. "You're going to give the seventh and eighth graders a run for their money! Good stuff!"

I don't know about "good stuff," but at least I've determined that butterflies aren't as boring as I thought they were.

Or at least I can accept that monarchs are cool. Other butterflies are still tarantula food.

It's a myth that if a butterfly loses the "powder" from its wings, it will be unable to fly. The "powder" is made up of microscopic scales that *do* affect flight, but butterflies can still function after losing some. Researchers handle them minimally and very gently, and when necessary, they simply fold the butterfly's wings into their closed position and place the butterfly in an envelope to prevent more scale loss during transportation.

The Homefront

Tonight when I got home, I planned to head straight upstairs and start working on my part of the project. But when I opened the door, all thoughts of homework were drowned out by a smell from the kitchen that was quickly turning from toasted to burnt.

Mom was fanning something in a cast-iron skillet on the stove. Izzy was rolling stuff out on the table between sheets of parchment paper. It looked like balls of white Play-Doh.

"What are you doing?" I asked.

Mom said that she'd decided to try and make flour tortillas. I was dumbfounded.

"*You* can make tortillas?"

"Well, yes. Or at least *other people* can make tortillas. I can make—what did you call them, Izzy?"

"Flat goo balls. Wait," she said, eyeballing the skillet. "*Blackened* flat goo balls." If there's one thing my sister is good at, it's complaining.

"This shouldn't be this hard," Mom muttered as she pried a charred tortilla from the pan and chucked it into the trash, where it landed on top of about six other ones.

This seemed like a lot of effort for something we usually just buy, so I said, "You've never made tortillas before."

"I was thinking maybe I'd actually make the tortillas for Great-Auntie Fortuna's carnitas quesadillas for our Day of the Dead ofrenda this year. She always made her own tortillas, right up until the day she died, and I've been feeling guilty about using store-bought ones. But judging by today's results, I'll need a lot of practice. Or maybe we'll put one of her other favorite foods by her picture on the family altar this year. We can remember her through other foods, right?"

"That's a really good idea," I said. "I think we should remember Great-Auntie Fortuna by sharing ofrenda food with her that falls under the category of sweet and doughy!"

Just then, Dad walked in. One sniff and a look in the trash can, and he suggested going out for dinner.

Mom has given up on her "we don't eat stuff in restaurants that we can make at home" rule since we moved to Dallas. I don't remember any places in ~~Belle~~ The Place Not Named that could compete with Mom's cooking. But Dallas has so many places that are good, even she has agreed we can eat out more. So I guess that's one point for Dallas.

I was hoping for Greek food, but Mom wanted to find a place with fresh house-made tortillas that she could buy if her own didn't get any better before Day of the Dead comes. So we went to a Mexican restaurant that was also a bakery. Dallas wins this point too because there are so many different kinds of bakeries here. We were lucky there was one bakery back in The Place Not Named. But here, there are *waaaay* more options to pick from.

Anyway, the bakery tonight still had some pan dulce left for sale, even though it was late in the day, and some tortillas too. I also saw a sign that they do the traditional pan de muerto for Day of the Dead. I reminded Mom of how much Great-Auntie Fortuna loved pan dulce and sweets, and she let me fill an entire bag with baked stuff so we could "taste test" them for the ofrenda.

When we got home, we cut everything in half and then shoveled it in our faces. I picked conchas with yellow sugar all over the top, pineapple cake, and some puff-pastry things. They were all GREAT! I wonder how much space will be on the altar in our new living room? I hope there's enough to offer Great-Auntie Fortuna ALL the things we tried tonight.

After dessert, Mom announced to everyone that we'd be ramping up our efforts for our celebration of Day of the Dead.

"Dad's family doesn't celebrate it," she said, "and my side of the family has only been celebrating this holiday since the mid-eighties. I always wondered if we were missing out on any parts of it. So now that we're in a place where there are a lot of people who celebrate it, I want to really explore it."

"Day of the Dead starts the day after Halloween. If we do more for it, will we still get to do Halloween?" asked Izzy.

"Of course we will," said Mom. "It's an entirely different holiday with a whole different purpose. Day of the Dead is like Memorial Day, a time to remember the people we loved, and—"

"And that's why we put so much thought into how we decorate the ofrenda," I said, reciting Mom's usual Day of the Dead speech, "and why we choose the foods we share with their spirits, because—"

"It's all to remember them and celebrate their lives," finished Izzy.

Mom laughed and said, "YES! And now that we live in Dallas, it won't be just us and a few other families celebrating Day of the Dead. There are several different community events around the area. So we'll do our usual Halloween thing, and then Day of the Dead this year will involve lots more activities!"

I was pretty excited about Day of the Dead this year, but then Mom turned to me and said, "I've been doing some reading, and guess what, Bertie? Day of the Dead ties in to your science project! Some people believe that monarch butterflies are their family members' souls returning for a visit on Day of the Dead. Isn't that beautiful?"

Argh! Even at home I can't escape those stupid butterflies! "Yeah, sure," I said, and then I rushed upstairs and decorated the outside of Worf's tank with a paper-printout backdrop of the rocks from the classic episode of *Star Trek: The Original Series* where Captain Kirk fights the Gorn lizard guy. I thought it was much better than spending more time talking about monarchs.

Studying the King

Mr. Eagon began our Science Squad meeting today by saying that this was OUR project and that his job was to give us the supplies, meeting space, and someone to ask questions of when we got stuck, but that we were in the driver's seat (Lyla smiled) and that he would not be doing any more teaching. It was all us from here forward.

We already knew from the handouts Mr. Eagon gave us that we'll log basic information for each tag we place about whether the butterfly was a male or a female, who tagged it, and the date and city where the butterfly was tagged. So Thurmond, Gavin, and Caden taught us what we'd need to know to be good at finding, collecting, and raising our butterflies.

Thurmond started off by showing us what the life cycle of a butterfly looks like. It includes four stages:

1. Egg

2. Larva

3. Pupa

4. Adult

Like many insects, butterflies change from eggs
to larvae to pupae before becoming adults. Thurmond
explained that caterpillars are the larval stage. And a
butterfly pupa is often called a chrysalis.

"Monarchs usually have a short life span of two to
six weeks," he said, "but hopefully the specimens we catch

will be part of that generation that is traveling south and will live for several months. We need to tag and release them by the end of October so they can safely fly south, if they will.

"But the devil is in the details. We don't know if the butterflies we'll catch will be part of that final journey, and we don't know how old they are. So we need to treat them like they have an expiration date. I think the more caterpillars and chrysalises we can raise, the better, since we at least know they have that minimum adult life span."

He said we'd have to keep the specimens in individual containers or cages, like plastic shoeboxes, cleaned and sterilized yogurt containers, or any clear container that we could put a screen covering onto to help airflow. We'd keep the specimens separate to prevent any diseased animals from infecting others. And we'd have to keep adults and chrysalises separate from caterpillars for the same reason. We would even have to clean out the cages daily and sterilize them regularly with a bleach solution.

"So if we're lookin' mostly for caterpillars right now, how do we know if a caterpillar we see is a monarch caterpillar?" asked Lyla.

"I'm sure Blurtie can answer that," said Thurmond, looking at me. I could tell he was hoping I'd be caught off guard.

"Oh, uh, they look like these examples," I said, pointing to Thurmond's pictures of the larval stage. "See, they're striped, with these protuberances—that means things that stick out—on each end. I'll talk more about identification in my part tomorrow."

"I can partly answer that question too," said Gavin, "because those caterpillars will basically only be found on milkweed plants."

Then Gavin taught us how to identify milkweed. Since milkweed is the only place monarch moms lay their eggs and the only food monarch caterpillars eat, it's also the best place to look for monarchs. Gavin showed us pictures of the areas where milkweed grows in Dallas— sort of open fields and prairies. Then he showed us pictures of green milkweed, the most common variety in Texas. It's about one to three feet high, and it has big leaves perfect for feeding caterpillars.

Thurmond confirmed that fact, as if he had to put a stamp of approval on everything that came up.

"Since we'll need milkweed to feed the caterpillars regularly, it's probably a good idea to collect some of the plants," said Gavin. "But be careful when you handle them—milkweed sap has a latex in it that is painful and can cause damage if it gets in your eyes!"

That sounded pretty bad, but Gavin said that really the worst thing about milkweed is that it's becoming scarce. Since it's thought of as a weed, people get rid of it or kill it off in gardens and farm areas and places like that. Now some monarch citizen science projects help make food and habitats for monarchs by growing and planting milkweed. People around Dallas, especially gardeners, are trying to plant it again too.

When Gavin was done, Caden told us about adult butterflies. They eat by drinking nectar from all sorts of wildflowers, so we will need to find fresh flowers for them every day too. Caden mentioned something about how we could make nectar for them from sugar and water, but that monarch scientists prefer feeding captive monarchs with flowers. Then he said pretty much the same upkeep stuff that Thurmond had said about separating and cleaning. Thurmond nodded his head and looked pretty pleased with himself.

"Wow," said Gavin, "this is a TON of work. No wonder scientists need help!"

We all nodded at that.

Finally, something I have in common with the rest of the Squad!

Finding and Capturing Targets

Today was Lyla's and my turn to teach. I'd come up with a great idea, and I thought I would really have something to offer the group. I worked out how to say it while Lyla got up and talked about tagging the "wily and elusive" monarch butterfly.

I was drinking a can of pop, and I almost blew it out of my nose when she said that. Like a butterfly could be wily and elusive! But what was even better was her description of how to catch them.

"You sneak up on butterflies just like you would if you were racing at the Texas Motor Speedway," she said. "You approach from behind the butterfly so it can't see you coming. You do it slow so that even if the butterfly had a rearview mirror to check, it wouldn't suspect anything. Any sudden movement in your approach will convince the driver you want to pass—I mean, the butterfly you want to catch—that there's something to worry about, and *vroom!* He'll take off. So you take it nice and easy, then lickety-split, you zip around him! Or in our case, you sweep the net forward and flip the end of the net bag back over the handle to trap it."

I pictured Lyla driving a race car behind a butterfly in a NASCAR car. Like this:

She went on to say that we should use quality nets, not those nets that come with kid butterfly kits because those are not usually long and deep enough and can hurt the butterflies. She described how we had to be really delicate when removing butterflies from the net bag, grasping them gently with their wings folded.

First, we'll put our thumb and pointer finger around the leading edge of the wings from the outside of the bag. Next, we'll use the other hand to reach into the bag and take them out, holding them with the same two fingers. Then, we'll gently put the tag on the mitten-shaped area on the underside of the hindwing.

"I'm going to excel at this," said Thurmond. "You guys know I'm very good at working on robotics and handling tiny wires and connections on motherboards. You can see all the badges I have for those things on the Science Squad website."

The competitive side of me flared up. "I should be pretty good at this too. You have to handle tarantulas very gently, and I'm really good with Worf."

Lyla smiled, but Thurmond just frowned.

"Yeah, well, I'm gonna suck at this," Caden said, "I've got total ham hands." He laughed. "Get it, *ham* hands? You know, because . . . barbecue?" We all groaned.

"Here's the thing," said Lyla. "Kids actually have an advantage over adults in this particular kind of citizen science. We have smaller hands than adults, and that makes it easier for us to apply tags. Everyone hold up your hands."

We all did and looked around.

"Whoa," said Caden, looking at me. "Bertie's hands are tiny."

"Yeah," Thurmond said, "they're not nearly as big as his mouth."

People make fun of other people for a lot of different reasons. Funky hobbies (collecting dog hair!), strange pets (earwigs!), lack of hygiene (BO!), but I never realized that hands could be one of them. But Caden was right. My hands seemed shrunken and pitiful compared to the others—except Lyla's, which were about the same size as mine.

"Don't listen to them, Bertie," Lyla said. "That just means you'll be our champion tagger."

Caden nudged Gavin, and he snorted. Thurmond had a strange look on his face, sort of like he was mad. He kept looking at my hands, and then his, and then back at Lyla.

Well, at least the Squad will have some use for keeping me around. But I hope this doesn't turn into a nickname too.

It was finally my turn to explain how to identify monarchs. We didn't have monarchs in The Place Not

Named, so it felt weird telling people how to identify something when I'd never actually seen it, but it was pretty simple.

I explained that monarchs are like the royalty of butterflies because they are big for butterflies. An adult monarch's wings can be around four inches wide. Since we had to record whether each butterfly we caught was male or female, I'd concentrated on that identification fact the most. All monarchs are orange and black with white spots on the outer edges of their wings. Male monarchs have a black dot on each hindwing. Females seem slightly darker than males, and their black lines are thicker.

I described the caterpillars too. They're white, black, and greenish-yellow striped, with protuberances on each end. They grow from less than a half inch to beasts nearly two inches long.

My part felt really short. But at least I had a plan to end with a bang.

"We will need to finish tagging and releasing our butterflies by the end of October," I said, "because all the butterflies either migrate by then or die when the cold weather hits, which gave me an idea."

"Great," whispered Caden, "this is the part where he tells us that he thinks it would be a grand idea to feed any dead ones to poor, starving tarantulas."

"No," I said, heating behind my ears. Then I told them about how monarchs link to Day of the Dead. "I was thinking we could keep some of the butterflies we collect and tag. Then we could let them go all at once at the Day of the Dead Festival. It would help increase awareness about monarch migration and their declining numbers. And we can even show people what we're doing as citizen scientists to help. It'll be so cool that other people will want to go out and do what we do!"

There was silence in the room.

Then Lyla spoke. "Oh my gosh, Bertie. What a great idea!"

"You know, there's a Best of the Booths award at the festival. If we won that, we'd sure make an impression on the judges, which could help us beat the seventh- and eighth-grade Squads," said Thurmond.

"Not bad, new guy," said Gavin.

Maybe things are finally looking up for me in the Squad.

(*Also, there's no way I'd feed monarch caterpillars to Worf! According to my research, the milkweed they eat makes them taste terrible to predators.*)

Evading Capture

We've started searching for monarchs, but we haven't caught any specimens yet because in order to catch them, you have to find them first. I've spotted several milkweed plants, but they haven't had any caterpillars on them.

Thurmond told the Squad he was going to catch the most monarchs. I think that was a challenge, but the reality is that we ALL have to catch a lot if we're going to make any kind of impression at the festival and beat the other Squads. I wonder if there's a sticker for gathering specimens? It would be nice to have a different sticker to add to my collection on my profile page—especially since Thurmond keeps bragging about how he already has *five*.

I watched for butterflies this weekend in our backyard because there are flowers out there, and butterflies need huge amounts of nectar to fuel up for the long flight to Mexico. But the few butterflies I've seen always pass our yard and go over the fence into the yard of the cranky lady next door. Mom and Dad were very specific about not bothering her, so butterflies are out of the question once they cross that fence. I tried to catch them before that happened, but they kept getting away. You'd think butterflies would be easy to catch, but they move fairly fast. I didn't get any.

Disaster at
the Homefront

Today, while I was "watching" Izzy for Mom and Dad,
I sat out back again, hoping for a bunch of butterflies
to magically land in our yard. After what felt like forever,
I finally saw a big black-and-orange one heading for
the sunflowers in the corner. I didn't get a close enough
look to tell if it was a monarch butterfly, but that
doesn't matter to me. I'm going to try and catch every
butterfly that might be a monarch because I don't want
to waste time trying to ID the thing before I snag it.
I'm worried it will hear me coming and fly away.

I was applying my best techniques in the stealthy
pursuit of the butterfly when I heard a shriek and a
squeal in the kitchen.

Dropping my net, I ran inside to see Izzy covered
in white bubbles, trying to stop a tide of foam that
swirled out of the partly open dishwasher. I ran over to
help her close the door, but I slipped and fell face-first

into a cluster of bubbles on the floor. After much sliding and skidding, I finally managed to right myself, shuffle my way to the dishwasher, and shut it. It burbled and groaned and made weird noises like it was chewing up all of our dishes.

I turned to my sister. "What happened? Are you okay?"

She fluffed the suds between her hands and tried to sculpt it into a shape. "I tried to help with the dishes. The dishwasher started making funny noises, so I opened it to look, and all this fluff started coming out. Isn't it pretty?" She blew some off her elbow.

I looked at the counter and saw an empty bottle of dish soap—the kind you use to wash dishes by hand. She must have used it in the dishwasher instead of dishwasher detergent.

"Izzy!" I yelled, grabbing my head and spitting out a few choice Klingon curse words so Izzy wouldn't recognize what I said and get me in trouble later. "Look at this mess! We've gotta clean this up before Mom and Dad get home."

"Is it going to be okay?" she asked, pointing to the belching dishwasher.

I told her I was pretty sure she'd killed it. Then I turned it off.

We started cleaning up the kitchen, but Izzy started laughing every time a clump of bubbles puffed into the air as we scooped them up and tried to rinse them down the sink. My elbow and forehead hurt, I was covered in dish soap, and I was starting to itch. I was in no mood for humor.

"Will you be serious?" I snarled. "This is not funny!"

"Actually, it is!"

"No, it isn't!"

"Yes, it is!"

We went on like this for a while, with Izzy doing way more arguing than cleaning. Eventually, the kitchen was pretty much spotless, but I did ~~most of~~ pretty much all of the work. I was still mad when I took Izzy outside to hose her off, so I turned the water up higher until she squealed and it shot over the fence.

The lady next door came to the fence and complained loudly that her yellow goldenrod, asters, and decorative thistle really didn't need to be watered. She didn't look at us, but I realized this was a hint. So I dragged Izzy inside to dry off.

The butterfly was long gone by then.

Later, Mom and Dad laughed when Izzy and I described what had happened. They weren't even mad, since it turned out the dishwasher was fine once they ran it for two cycles to clear the suds, and the kitchen floor is REALLY clean now.

I don't know what made me angrier—losing what could have been my first butterfly or the fact that Izzy didn't even get in trouble.

But there's no way Izzy can get in the way every day, so catching butterflies can only get easier (I hope).

Monarchs actually don't hear very well, so they use their other senses to get information about their world. Adult butterflies get most of their ability to smell through their antennae, and while they use a long tongue-like body part called a proboscis to sip nectar, they actually have tasting organs on their feet!

The Search for the King

At the Squad meeting today, I found out that I'm not the only one having problems finding and catching monarchs. I really thought these butterflies would be everywhere based on what everyone said, but they aren't. I've only spotted a few and haven't caught ANY. But at least I'm not alone—Gavin hasn't caught any, either. Thurmond brought in three caterpillars, Caden found one, and Lyla found one butterfly. She has a bruise on her forehead from it—the catching, not the butterfly itself. Apparently, it startled her while she was under a truck with her dad, changing oil. And she was so excited, she bonked her forehead against the running board of the truck when she scooted out to follow the butterfly.

Butterfly hunting is dangerous. Who knew?

The other Squads also planned to have booths at the fair (copycats!), and the judges decided to have all the booths do scheduled presentations. I know I wasn't the only one who had been thinking of the sight of lots of butterflies being released at the festival and how much attention that would bring to scientists' questions about monarch migration and their concern about the recent drop in numbers. I'm still not saying butterflies are as cool as tarantulas, but that would be something to see, and like Thurmond said, something that cool might give us an edge over the other Squads.

But to do that, we would need a LOT more specimens.

We printed a map of Dallas and marked all the places we'd looked and where we'd seen or caught butterflies or found caterpillars. We looked for patterns, but there didn't seem to be any at all. Even Thurmond didn't have any suggestions about places to collect specimens. He said his success so far was because he is always looking for butterflies, and then he went back to scribbling in his journal.

"Maybe we could grow our own plants?" Caden suggested.

"Growing milkweed from seeds takes months, which is way more time than we have," said Gavin. "And we can't afford to buy grown plants."

So we looked through our books and sources on the internet and made a more specific list of places to find milkweed. It grows in less populated or unpopulated areas, like:

- prairies
- pastures along the roadside or railroad tracks
- vacant lots
- dry hillsides
- dry pine barrens (a barren is like an open-ish flat area with smaller pine trees and shrubs all over it—I had to look it up)

Milkweed also grows near parks and wild spaces that might have these kinds of places, like the Great Trinity Forest. I laughed when we listed that. Dallas, the *city*, couldn't possibly have a REAL forest.

I stopped laughing when Lyla said she read somewhere that the Great Trinity Forest, which is just on the southern edge of Dallas, is the largest hardwood forest in the country. I'm not sure I believe it, but I don't think Lyla would make that up.

So we have a more specific list of places to search. We also decided we'd wait to tag our butterflies until right before they are released, just in case any die.

That way, we don't waste time tagging monarchs that won't migrate. Between planning the booth, preparing our presentation, and caring for the specimens, we have a lot of work to do. But so far, finding and catching specimens is the hardest part!

WHERE ARE THEY HIDING?

Still Searching . . .

Gavin brought in five caterpillars today, so now I'm the only Squad member who hasn't found any. He'd figured his brothers saw more prairies and pastures and roadsides than anyone, so he'd shown them how to spot milkweed and collect caterpillars. On Thursday, they were out storm chasing in the northeastern part of Texas. Luckily, when they stopped on the side of a road to figure out where the storm was headed, they recognized patches of milkweed under some power lines. They had managed to find a few caterpillars and gather some milkweed plants before the storm shifted toward them. They'd saved the caterpillars from the storm and helped our project!

Gavin put all his caterpillars in one big plastic aquarium with a light mesh lid so they'd have lots of space and air. This was totally fine since we'd learned that we could keep up to ten specimens together in a large container. These had already been living together on the same plant, and it would make cleanup and feeding easier, since we have to change gloves between specimen containers when we're dealing with them.

We were all excited to see them. Since they're bigger caterpillars, that means they'll probably become butterflies in time for the Day of the Dead Festival at the beginning of November!

Gavin talked more about how the place where his brothers found the caterpillars looked. According to their notes, it was something along the lines of "lots of dark skies above, a few power lines to watch, winds mostly heading southeast in an open-ish dry field with a farmhouse."

In other words, there wasn't much we could use from that to find other spots. Not to mention it was *waaaay* out in the middle of nowhere.

I feel like the monarchs are hiding from us. Where are they?

Even More Searching. . .

<u>Pick Your Own Path:</u>

Your landing party has searched the entire alien city for the king, but you have not found him. You:

<u>A.</u> Decide to name yourself Ultimate Supreme King of the Planet. Turn to Page 51. Page 51: Your local supporters are confused by your claim, since the words *ultimate* and *supreme* translate in their language as "pencil holder." They give you the job of being King of Those Who Wield Pencils, which isn't so bad because it turns out that Those Who Wield Pencils are writers who are treated like rock stars. You get your own sci-fi TV show and lots of sponsorships and live happily ever after.

<u>B.</u> Go search every building again and find a freshly dug tunnel labeled "Outpost" in the basement of a building. You follow it. Turn to Page 5. Page 5: You follow the tunnel deep into the planet, but right as you reach the king, you're both captured by another species

of creature that kicks you both off the planet in a spacepod. You are doomed to spend eternity floating in space with the king, whose breath always smells like salami.

C. Give up and return home in disgrace.

I don't know how much more butterfly hunting I can take. If I don't find one soon, I might have to pick C.

King Catcher

I found a monarch caterpillar this morning on the way to school! Mom treated us to breakfast from the Mexican bakery. I liked it so much, it could make me start actually liking Texas. Anyway, I noticed some milkweed growing in the vacant lot next door. I found a caterpillar under one of the leaves, so I collected it in a clean, empty travel mug from the car (I should probably start carrying my specimen-collecting stuff with me).

I dropped the caterpillar off in the lab before my first class, and I was really excited to show it to the Squad in our meeting today, but when I got there, my single caterpillar could not compare to the *TWENTY-FIVE* containers Thurmond brought in.

The containers Thurmond used were made from thick plastic, about the same size and shape as cottage cheese or sour cream containers, except these were partly see-through plastic, with a piece of mesh over the top held on with a rubber band. He set them on the shelves in the lab, where we could kind of see the thick, striped bodies and leaves inside each one.

"Wow! Those are all monarchs?" asked Caden.

Thurmond nodded with an air of superiority.

"Are you sure?" said Gavin. "There's so many!"

Thurmond glanced in the top of the nearest container, then handed it to me. "*You're* the expert, Blurtie. What do *you* think?" He narrowed his eyes.

I took a deep breath and looked in the top through the mesh at the caterpillar. It was mostly hidden under a milkweed leaf, but each end sticking out the sides of the leaf had a set of protuberances. And the parts I could see had greenish-yellow, black, and white stripes. I suppose I could have pulled it out to get a really good look at it, but I didn't want to handle any of the caterpillars too much.

I held up the container above my head like a trophy. "We have monarchs!"

For once, everyone cheered and clapped when I said something!

It felt good.

Thurmond nodded with satisfaction and put the container back on the shelf.

"How'd you find all these?" asked Caden.

"My superior searching skills combined with an eye for detail," said Thurmond. "I told you I'd find the most specimens."

"The race isn't over yet, Thurmond," said Lyla.

"True," he said, smiling at her. "I could take you with me sometime, show you how it's done."

"Oh, uh, thanks, but my and Bertie's parents have agreed on a schedule to take us out collecting—you know, since we live near each other—and we can't really change that now . . ."

I had no idea what she was talking about, but the slightly nervous side-glance she gave me told me it was my turn to help her.

"So where'd you find them?" I asked—to change the subject and because I was seriously wondering how he had found so many.

"I found them out at a park near Fort Worth when I went to visit my grandma. I thoroughly checked every plant I saw and collected all the specimens and lots of milkweed, so there's no point in going back."

That sounded kind of suspicious to me, but I didn't want to ruin the feeling of being accepted. Plus, Fort

Worth is nearly an hour's drive away, so it's not like any of us would go there just to check for monarchs.

We cleaned up after our specimens and fed them. When we left the science room, Lyla pulled me aside in the hall.

"Bertie, something smells fishy about this whole thing," she said.

"It might be my backpack—it smells a little funny lately. Maybe it's getting stinky from all the sweat I work up while I'm looking for specimens."

"Bertie! I'm serious!"

"Okay, okay," I said. "I know what you're thinking: *How is one person finding so many specimens so fast?* There are five of us looking, and we'd barely scraped together a dozen as of this morning. Then, suddenly, Thurmond shows up with twenty-five! It's like a pick-your-own-path story: Your ship's pilot claims he single-handedly shot down seventy-three enemy ships, but no one actually saw him do it. You—"

Lyla cut me off. "Bertie, if you spent as much time collecting as you do thinking up alternate versions of things, we'd have found way more monarchs to tag by now."

"Yeah, maybe," I said, laughing. "Hey, what was that whole 'schedule' thing?"

For the first time, I saw Lyla look totally uncomfortable. "Well, I just couldn't figure out how to politely tell him I do *not* want to spend any time with him 'teaching' me about his superior searching skills. Can you imagine? Actually, don't. Bleh!"

"Of course I can imagine, but you just told me not to." I dodged as she took a swing at my shoulder. "Maybe it's good not to have too many specimens yet," I said. "More specimens means more to clean up after and feed every day, and I'm not exactly looking forward to cleaning up more frass." (*Frass* is the scientific term for insect poop).

She laughed. "Yep, those little caterpillars are champion poop-makers!"

Once again, I imagined how cool it would be to have a TON of monarchs to let go—we'd fill the sky with orange and black like a whole tornado of migration. I bet at least Gavin would like that.

But my mental picture of the tornado of butterflies was ruined because suddenly, every single one had a label on it that said "Found by Thurmond."

Maybe Lyla does have a point. It seems strange that one person could find so many butterflies, even someone as ~~crazy~~ dedicated as Thurmond. Where is he getting them?

??? Suspicions Arise

I'm even more sure now that Thurmond couldn't possibly have found all those butterflies. This is REALLY hard!

Every little blip of orange and black on a flower sends me running and then sneaking up on the insect and nabbing it. Or every time I see something that resembles milkweed, I have the urge to go turn over every leaf to see if there is a caterpillar underneath.

This morning, the neighbor lady caught me inspecting one of the flowers on her side of the yard between our front porches. There always seem to be things flying around her flowers, and today, I saw something black and orange. By the time I got to the plant, the butterfly had flown into her backyard, and right as I was about to stand up, she flung the door open. It's a good thing I had my lucky space pen in my hand (the one where the spaceship moves from one end to the other when you tilt it, not the one that writes upside down, underwater, and

85

in zero gravity). When she came out on her porch, I bent farther down and pretended to be picking it up.

"Oh, here it is," I said loudly, hoping she'd think I was just looking for my pen.

"You aren't taking anything from my yard, are you?" she asked, glaring at me suspiciously.

"No ma'am. Just looking for my pen."

"You make sure that's all you're looking for," she said and then went inside and slammed the door.

What would she be so worried about in her yard that she thinks I'd take? Does she have buried treasure out there or something? Who knows? Maybe there's something that she doesn't want me to find, like a dead body buried under all of her flowers, or a secret bunker. But that mystery will have to wait until I have more butterflies.

How does Thurmond find so many of them? I've hardly found any at all, even though it seems like every moment I'm not doing homework, I'm trying to convince my parents to go to a park or drive around looking for weeds in public areas. Although I have to admit, that isn't entirely about butterflies. It may also be about finding important Dallas food landmarks.

Insect Imposters

Here's a new idea for a pick-your-own-path book:

Pick Your Own Path:

A field near the park where you came to search for caterpillars and butterflies has high grass that may be hiding several venomous snakes. According to your search partner, the snakes may not take too kindly to you walking through their home and startling them. Bites are possible, but just on the other side of the field, there are several flowering plants that look like they are covered in butterflies. You:

<u>A.</u> Figure you are a tough guy and wade through the grass. Turn to page 30. Page 30: You are bitten by a new species of snake with laser vision made by scientists in a secret military lab, which it escaped by burning a hole through its cage and then came here to this field. As the venom rushes through your body, you sense that you are changing, and you realize you've

become a snake yourself. You spend the rest of your life in the field, zapping and eating rats.

<u>B.</u> Decide this is just too hard and give up your dream of becoming a scientist, starting now. Turn to page 64. Page 64: You stop paying attention in school and doing homework and have to repeat school over and over again. You finally graduate from high school at age ninety-three—which would be great, except you can't remember what school you went to, so you show up at the wrong graduation ceremony and never actually get your diploma.

<u>C.</u> Decide to rely on your partner. Turn to page 72. Page 72: Your partner brought along her remote-control truck and strapped an old video camera on a tripod in the bed of the truck. She sends the truck through the field and gets closer to the bushes.

It could totally happen, all of it. Of course, I had choice C.

When the truck approached the bushes, Lyla maneuvered it and the camera near some of the butterflies. The camera jiggled a bit as she got used to handling it.

"This is harder than I expected. All the weight in the back completely throws off the steering," said Lyla, twiddling the controls. "I'm going to drive around under the bush so we can see under the leaves for caterpillars, then I'll pull back to see those butterflies."

"Can you get a steady enough picture to see if those are monarchs?" I asked.

She drove the camera around the bushes and back, and then we took the camera off the truck to look at the video. The camera did get a fairly decent look at the butterflies. "This looks like a monarch from the side," she said.

The butterfly opened and closed its wings. When its wings were closed, it looked just like a monarch. But when it opened its wings, it was clearly some other kind of butterfly. It was orange and black, but it had a different pattern.

"Dang it!" I said. "What kind of butterfly is that?"

I pulled the identification guide out of my backpack, flipped through the pages, and found the butterfly that looked like the one in the video. It was a queen butterfly. Apparently, there are a bunch of butterflies that look similar to monarchs. They all have sort of royal or castle-like names too: queen, viceroy, and soldier.

"What in the heck is a viceroy?" Lyla asked.

I looked at description in the book. "A viceroy is an official who rules in locations other than a home country or base of power on behalf of a monarch," I read. "Huh, it's like a substitute. I can see why they'd name them that way—they could totally substitute for a monarch butterfly," I said, pointing to the page.

We didn't see any monarchs anywhere else we looked today either. But it was still a good day because Lyla let me drive the truck, and I only got it stuck under a bush once. It was right next to a paved path, so I could see that there were no venomous snakes to get in the way of rescuing the truck.

I read more about the look-alikes after dinner. I hadn't even thought to look for information about those when I was researching how to identify monarchs. It's a good thing I looked again. Not only do their adult forms look like monarchs but some of the caterpillar forms do too, and some even eat milkweed like monarchs. I've drawn some of the look-alikes and how they are different from monarchs on the next page.

VICEROY

MONARCH

QUEEN

MONARCH   VICEROY   QUEEN

I felt a little guilty, reading the butterfly book in front of Worf's cage. I wonder if it made her hungry. I offered her a cricket as a consolation prize, but she didn't seem interested, the picky eater!

Space Aliens
and Limb Count

I was totally distracted by two tests and a project this morning, but when Lyla and I were eating lunch today, it suddenly hit me: I remembered the caterpillar look-alike thing.

"Lyla, what if Thurmond's caterpillars were all imposters?" I said. "I did more reading last night, and it turns out that queen caterpillars look a lot like monarch caterpillars too. They're both striped in black, white, and greenish-yellow. It might explain how he found so many!"

"Maybe," she said. "Oh wait, no—none of us knew there were other butterflies that look so much like monarchs in all stages of life. So if that's the case, wouldn't we all be finding lots of queen caterpillars too? We'd all have tons of specimens. Despite Thurmond's claim about his 'superior searching skills,' it still doesn't explain why he's the only one finding them."

"You're right," I said. Then another thought occurred to me. "Oh, man. I'm the one who looked at his specimens and said they were monarchs. What if all of our specimens are the wrong ones? Everyone's gonna hate me—I mean, hate me *more*."

"The guys don't hate you. Y'all just got off on the wrong foot."

"I'm pretty sure Thurmond doesn't like me much. And I'll bet he's deliberately cheating somehow and getting help finding caterpillars."

"Careful, Bertie," Lyla said. "We can't really prove anything."

"Yet," I said.

Is it mean that I really wanted Thurmond to be cheating and to catch him? He's been a jerk, but I guess Lyla's right. Bringing in the wrong caterpillars wouldn't mean he *meant* to bring in imposters. But I'm still kind of (just a tiny little bit) looking forward to seeing his face if his specimens aren't monarchs. I asked Lyla not to tell the guys if she got to the Squad meeting before I did, 'cause I want to do it.

Then, right after school, I had a last-minute meeting with Ms. Finch about my language arts fiction project.

She wants to use my story in the new school magazine she's putting together—which is pretty cool, but I was so excited about telling the Squad about look-alike caterpillars that I haven't had a chance yet to think much about it. She just kept going on and on about the magazine, and I was about to interrupt her when she finally let me go.

After leaving Ms. Finch's room, I sprinted down the stairs and hall to the other end of the building and almost ran into the Squad in the hall outside the cafeteria.

"Oh, hey," said Caden. "We just finished cleaning and feeding. We did your specimens too, because we thought you were never coming."

I said thanks, then I quickly told them about caterpillar imposters. They looked shocked. Except for Thurmond. He just looked worried.

"So we should check how many protuberances all our caterpillars have," I said. "A monarch has two sets, and a queen has three sets. The extra one is in the middle of the caterpillar's body."

We ran back to the classroom, but the lights were out, and the door was locked! Mr. Eagon must have left for the day.

We all agreed that first thing tomorrow, we'd find out what kind of specimens we have in the lab. I'm torn—I really wish that Thurmond's are all imposters . . . but then that makes me look stupid too. If they are all monarchs, that's better for our project . . . but then I'll have to see that smug smile on Thurmond's face again. I don't know which is worse.

Bodies of Evidence

I arrived at the lab this morning before school started, ready to inspect every specimen we had. Thurmond was already there, glumly stacking a few of his containers. Which were empty. I looked at the cages and containers, and most of the other specimens were gone too!

"Thurmond, where are the specimens?" Right as I said it, the rest of the Science Squad appeared, standing in the doorway.

"What's up, guys?" asked Gavin.

"There're a bunch of specimens missing. Most, in fact." I pointed to the cages. Everyone looked in the cages, double-checking my discovery.

"Thurmond was here first," I said, turning to him again. "What happened?"

He sniffled, and I noticed The Khaki Kid looked worn out and tired. All his superior searching must really be taking a toll on him. That, or he was up all night worrying about the specimens too.

"I came in early today to eat breakfast in the cafeteria and study for a test," he said. "But first I went straight to the science lab to check the caterpillars and found most of our specimens were dead. I didn't want them to contaminate the rest, so to save the others, I got rid of the dead ones immediately."

I felt kind of bad for him because only Thurmond's first three caterpillars, Lyla's butterfly, and Gavin's five caterpillars were left. That meant Thurmond's twenty-five specimens were gone. Caden's and mine were gone too.

"These are all monarchs," said Lyla inspecting the survivors.

"Did you see if the dead caterpillars were monarchs or queens?" I asked Thurmond.

He shook his head. "I panicked," he said. "I threw them away in the cafeteria garbage because I wanted them as far away from the lab as possible."

Caden shook his head. "They're probably crushed under all the breakfast trash by now. We'll never know what they were."

"Well," said Lyla, "at least now we know what the monarch caterpillars look like, and we can correctly identify them."

My thoughts went back and forth. Thurmond could be telling the truth. But it was REALLY convenient that the specimens died just as we were about to find out if they were imposters. This would be a perfect way to cover up any cheating. But I couldn't investigate any more since we all had to go to our first-period classes.

In the Squad meeting that afternoon, we talked about the possible reasons the specimens died. Mr. Eagon told us not to feel too bad—he'd expected we would lose some. Apparently, it's very common. Still, it felt bad to lose basically all our specimens.

"Hey, maybe it's the . . . the . . . what do you call that protozoan thing, again?" said Gavin.

"You mean the OE parasite?" said Caden. "The infection rate of the monarchs in our flyway is less than eight percent, so it's pretty unlikely that's what got our specimens."

"Yeah, and even if they were sick when we collected them, we've all been cleaning the cages really well," said Lyla. "We use disposable gloves when we're handling everything and change gloves between handling containers."

"And we've been keeping the butterflies and caterpillars separate and making sure they aren't too crowded," I said. "So I don't think that's it, either."

"According to my notes," said Caden, "the chrysalis and adult stages are where you can sometimes see the damage from infection, but even then, only some infected animals show the black spots or brown, black, or gray discoloring that can signal OE infection. Usually, you only test adults for OE infection. So we probably couldn't even tell if our caterpillars were infected. But what did they look like, Thurmond?"

Thurmond shrugged. "I wouldn't say they were black or brown or gray." He opened his journal. "From *my* research, it could have been *anything*: extreme temperatures, OE, bacterial or viral infections, or even other kinds of parasites, like parasitic fly larvae."

"Maybe it's a problem with the food sources," said Caden. "Maybe something came in on them and made the caterpillars sick."

"I don't think that's it," said Lyla. "We followed all those strict instructions. We even soaked all our milkweed in that ten percent bleach solution for twenty minutes, and we thoroughly rinsed it before storing it and feeding it to the caterpillars."

Then I remembered the time my family drove next to a field where a small airplane was flying low over the other side. Mom and Dad quickly found another route to take so we wouldn't have to be near the field. When Izzy asked what was going on, they explained the plane was a crop duster, probably spraying pesticides, and it wasn't a good idea for us to be inhaling them. Even a little pesticide on a plant would be bad for a butterfly or caterpillar since pesticides exist to kill insects, even the scientifically interesting ones.

"Maybe the leaves have pesticides left on them, or the pesticides may have soaked into them and can't be washed off," I said. Then another thought jumped into my head. "Oh no! Maybe there are pesticides on the flowers we collect for the butterfly too!"

"So what can we do?" asked Lyla.

Thurmond shrugged again. He appeared to be thinking very hard, and he started writing in his journal.

"How about instead of wildflowers, we switch to cotton balls soaked in a solution of organic honey and water?" I said. "One of the books I read said that works as a food source for butterflies, and then we know it isn't full of pesticides. It won't solve everything, but it could help the one butterfly we have and any others we catch or have once our caterpillars have pupated and become adults."

Everyone nodded when I said that, and Caden said, "That's a really good idea, Bertie. We have tons of organic honey at home from experimenting on barbecue sauce. I'll ask if I can bring some in."

I felt that tingle of acceptance. It's just really sad that most of our specimens had to die for me to get an actual compliment from someone on the Squad besides Lyla!

Armed and Dangerous

I caught two monarch butterflies this morning in our backyard heading for the neighbor's flowers. I still wonder if she buried her life savings in the flower bed up front, or the body of some kid who stepped on a flower. Or maybe she just loves her flowers more than people. Maybe she's a mutant plant lady from another planet, and the flowers are her babies. There are so many possibilities.

We didn't have a meeting today, but all of us except Thurmond came to clean up cages and drop off new specimens. Caden had a butterfly too. (Or was it Gavin? I didn't really notice who actually brought it, and those two always seem to do everything together, so it's hard to tell whose it was.) Lyla had a big caterpillar.

It's a good thing that Caden brought in a whole jar of organic honey, because now we have four butterflies to feed!

We made the solution, thinning the honey with water and soaking cotton balls in it, and we placed one cotton ball in each butterfly container. Then we cleaned the caterpillars' containers and fed them too.

Keeping caterpillars fed is especially important because if they get too hungry, some of the bigger caterpillars might eat the tiny ones. Who knew butterflies were cannibals?! COOL!

Caden and Gavin were finally nice to me. We all joked around while we were cleaning and feeding. I wonder if going through the trauma of losing so much of our project just kind of brought us together? Whatever the reason, today was great.

Well, not completely great, because there's always tons of poop in those cages. But there is one upside to cleaning up after monarchs: They aren't one of the breeds of butterflies where the caterpillars perform "scatapulting." Get it? "Scat" (poop) + "catapulting" = "scatapulting." It means the caterpillars FLING THEIR POO up to forty times the length of their bodies! Some scientists think the caterpillars that do this, like skipper butterfly larvae, do it for cleanliness. They think the caterpillars are trying to get the poop as far away from their homes as they can. Other scientists think it might be a mechanism for protecting themselves from predators like wasps that are drawn to the smell of the frass.

If the planet were ever invaded by aliens, scientists could engineer giant mutant butterflies that could shoot down enemy spaceships. Like this:

I think I finally really like butterflies (and Texas too).

Sending Out an SOS

After dinner tonight, I decided to try and do some more investigating about the death of our caterpillars. I really don't want to lose so many specimens ever again.

A basic computer search at the library gave me a bunch of websites that pretty much said the same causes of caterpillar death we already knew about: parasites, bacterial infections, and viruses. Nothing seemed to narrow down the possibilities.

Then I thought maybe I should be looking for help finding more specimens in the first place. Mr. Eagon did say it was common to have some caterpillars die when you are raising monarchs, so this could happen again. If I could just find more, it wouldn't be so bad when it happens.

I searched for "finding monarch caterpillars in Dallas," thinking maybe I could find hints on where other people have seen them locally. I found a "butterfly enthusiast" website that had a forum just for Dallas that anyone could join. A couple of conversations popped up.

I scrolled through them, looking for new ideas, but there weren't any. Everyone reported that they were seeing few monarchs, if any. It made me sad. But what was even sadder was that it seemed like every question received an answer mentioning that you can buy caterpillars and butterflies from a commercial butterfly farm. Of course, the user who posted these answers was a professional butterfly farmer.

I found one post he answered from a few weeks back from a user named "CowboyFan" asking about where to find lots of monarch caterpillars in Dallas and tips on keeping them from dying.

The farmer, of course, offered the idea of starting with farm stock, and CowboyFan thought that was a GREAT idea. The farmer didn't have any monarchs when CowboyFan wanted them, since the only stock he had left was in the chrysalis phase, but he had other options available (like queen caterpillars!) and said they should talk in email for more detail. There were no more posts, so I assume that's what they did.

I'm glad we're focusing on educating people about monarchs, because there are a lot of butterfly people like CowboyFan who probably don't know that farmed butterflies released into the wild can hurt the wild population.

Oh well. I guess we just have to keep looking for more wild specimens so we can capture people's interest and teach them how to help monarchs without harming them.

FRAMED

Today was my day to bring Worf to show to the class. It was great—one kid actually fainted! When I was done freaking everyone out, I put her cage back in the lab to keep her safe. When I came to check on her at lunch, the lid was loose on her cage—which is weird, because I don't remember opening it any other time since I left the house this morning except for when I gave her water right after we got to school. I do remember locking the lid after that. And I'm pretty sure it was back on tight before science class started . . .

I stopped by to check on her again after school, heading straight to the lab so I'd get there a few minutes before our Squad meeting. But when I looked inside the lab, Worf's cage was open, and SHE WAS NOWHERE IN SIGHT. And apparently, my spider is great at pulling off mesh and other coverings on caterpillar and butterfly containers too, because EVERY SINGLE ONE WAS EMPTY.

I was standing there frozen, staring at the empty containers with a total sense of dread—for the missing specimens, for Worf being gone, and for the probable verbal beating I was going to take from the Squad. And just when they were starting to maybe like me!

All thoughts left my head as I tried to understand the scene in front of me. Of course, right then the rest of the Squad came in to do the daily ritual of cage cleaning, feeding, and recording any notes about changes. They were so excited, it made me cringe.

"What the heck? Where are the specimens? Did you do something with them, Bertie?" asked Gavin.

"I don't see Worf," said Lyla. "Bertie, where's Worf?"

I couldn't respond.

"Oh my GOD, Bertie, your dumb spider ate our experiment!" yelled Caden, peering into Worf's cage from ten feet away. "She's not in there?! *Where is she?*" he said quieter, inspecting the ceiling like he was expecting an invasion from space. Then he went out to the classroom, moving slowly, like he was walking on eggshells. He was looking all over as if he was trying to see the ceiling, walls, and floor all at once.

"NOT COOL!" said Gavin. "How are we going to replace the specimens? It's super hard to find them in

the first place, and it's even worse trying to capture the butterflies—they go everywhere, like tiny twisters! This is a category-five problem!"

Thurmond just shook his head and walked back out into the classroom.

"What's all the excitement about?" asked Mr. Eagon, coming into the lab. "Did one of your caterpillars already start a chrysalis?"

"Bertie's spider ate our project," said Gavin flatly.

I finally found my voice. "No, she didn't!"

I sounded defensive, but I couldn't help it. I was sure Worf didn't eat all the monarchs. But everyone else seemed to think she did. I get why—there were empty monarch containers and cages, and my gargantuan spider was gone from her own open cage.

I tried to sound logical, despite the panic rising as I searched the room for signs of Worf.

"It couldn't have been Worf," I said. "Tarantulas catch multiple prey at once, lumping them together in a feeding ball, called a bolus, that is spun from spider silk. The bolus that Worf would make from all those caterpillars and butterflies would have been huge— there were thirteen specimens! I don't see one loose specimen or bolus. I don't know where she could have put them. Also, I just don't think she'd open up all those containers. A tarantula's claws or fangs can get stuck in mesh—that's why her whole container is smooth plastic. Some tarantulas can chew through mesh, but Worf isn't a very aggressive hunter. And look, these mesh covers aren't even chewed, they're just pulled off. So she's innocent! And right now, I just want to find her."

Mr. Eagon said something that sounded like he was trying to make us all feel better without blaming me. I don't really know what he said—I was too busy wondering where my pet was and if she was okay. I cleared my head and listened.

"So we have a loose tarantula. Oddly, this isn't the first time I've said that. Bertie, I'll look in the classroom, if you would check in here in the lab please. Make sure you check the window—the latch isn't reliable, and sometimes, it's open." Mr. Eagon turned and opened the door to the classroom, where I could see Caden sitting cross-legged on top of a lab table, watching the floor like a space settler who just discovered that there were hordes of carnivorous space beavers about to break through the floor tiles.

Gavin left too, but Lyla stayed and helped look. I closed the lab door again.

The window was latched when I checked. Gulping, I got down on my hands and knees and looked for Worf in the darkest corners of the room. Even if you like spiders, searching behind things and possibly being surprised while looking for a tarantula in a dark room is still a little nerve-wracking. Lyla was a champ, barely even flinching when she'd look behind boxes in dark corners that would be perfect for a jump scare.

Lyla finally spotted Worf hiding on a shelf behind a box of Bunsen burners. She poked me and made a motion toward the wall, saying nothing, like she thought Worf might hear us and run for another hidey-hole.

I managed to coax Worf into a new plastic cup from a supply shelf. I covered the top of the cup with a piece of cardboard while I moved to Worf's cage, just like I do at home. Then I put the cup in the cage so she could exit it when she was ready, and I locked the lid tight.

When we went back into the classroom, I told Mr. Eagon that Worf was found and contained. Everyone looked almost as relieved as I felt.

"I can't believe your spider ate everything we had left, even the new ones," said Caden.

I took a deep breath. "I told you, she couldn't have done it! She wasn't even hungry! If you overfeed a tarantula, they gorge, and then it's okay for them to not eat for a while. They're just full. She ate a huge amount of crickets just yesterday, so that's the state she was in when I brought her to school—FULL. So the idea that she could eat that many monarchs is kind of insane."

Mr. Eagon suggested that I take her home since we were running a project that made such an irresistible buffet available for her to sample. Even *he* thinks she did it! I took her cage and left without saying anything else.

Alone in Space

I really don't think Worf did it. The problem is that I have no idea why our specimens vanished. These are the only reasons I could think of:

- Space aliens beamed the caterpillars out for their own (surely nefarious) experiment (see below).
- Monarch butterflies do not actually migrate; they just mature super fast when no one is looking and teleport to their winter roosting sites.
- The lab has a magic pocket of "folding space" that our specimens got sucked into.
- Something else ate them or let them go.

So now we have to catch some more caterpillars and butterflies, and I have to find out who (or what) really took the caterpillars. At least things can't get worse. Not one of the guys from Science Squad would acknowledge me in the lunchroom today.

So much for impressing the class with Worf—I'm pretty sure everyone hates her. And me. Well, except for Lyla. Lyla was nice enough to continue to take pity on me and still be my friend. Which is good, because she keeps me from being completely alone. Everyone is calling her "Flyin' Lyla" now, although she'll probably never have to fly for her pudding again. She invented this magnet thing to attach to her pudding cups so they'll stick to her lunch box, which (of course) is a metal toolbox. And none of the drones the seventh-grade Squad has are strong enough to lift her toolbox.

Still, she's not a posse, a crew, or a group. I want a whole crowd, and that's not going to happen now. Most of the Squad thinks I screwed everything up for everyone. Now we have nothing to present in our booth at the Day of the Dead Festival, nothing to inspire people to help the monarchs, and no chance to beat the seventh- and eighth-grade Squads! I doubt I'll earn that education sticker now.

What if I upset Lyla too? It's a good thing I can work alone when needed.

<u>Pick Your Own Path:</u>

On your hiking trip to find the old ghost town, you screw everything up for yourself by upsetting all your potential friends. You:

<u>A.</u> Realize you can't live without them and try to make up. Turn to page 32. Page 32: You light a bonfire and have a mass apology and sing "Kumbaya."

<u>B.</u> Decide you are better off without them. Turn to page 65. Page 65: You get lost in the woods, and you're eaten by angry albino cave weasels.

<u>C.</u> Quit trying to bond with people who will never like you and ~~go back home where you have Jack, Dawson, and a lot of other friends!~~ close the book.

MORE Problems

At the Squad meeting today, we discussed how to find more monarchs. Actually, the rest of the Squad discussed it. I tried not to say anything. My stomach has been hurting ever since Worf ~~escaped~~ was framed, and anything I say will just make my life worse at this point.

We (they) didn't come up with anything new. Lyla tried to give us a pep talk to get us excited to go out and keep searching. It didn't work.

Then, it was like Thurmond read my mind, because he said, "Basically, we're not going to have anything to show at the Day of the Dead Festival. We can't earn our stickers or badges, and we have no chance at beating the other Squads."

I plopped my head down on the table. That was stupid, because then both my head *and* my stomach really hurt.

"But Lyla's right: We just gotta keep trying," he went on. "I think a truly knowledgeable and hardworking person would find a lot of butterflies no matter how hard they are to find."

"Well, if someone can find a huge mass of butterflies at this point, they'd be my hero for ever and ever," said Lyla.

Thurmond raised his eyebrows.

"Really?" I asked, lifting my head and snorting. "That's all it takes? Someone just finds a bunch of insects, and you think he or she is a hero?"

"Yep," said Lyla. "Badges and booths and beating seventh and eighth graders aren't really what this is about. This is about science and helping those scientists solve the mystery of monarch migration—and about getting more people involved so they can collect even more data. So yes," she batted her eyelashes and clasped her hands together by her face, "that person would be my hero!" She laughed.

"That person has to do a lot of work to get your attention," said Thurmond, sighing.

"We have more bad news," said Caden, shifting in his chair. "Our butterfly tags accidentally went through the paper shredder."

"WHAT?!" Lyla and I yelled at the same time.

The guys explained how someone had moved the sheets of the tag stickers to the wrong stack of papers in the lab room. When Gavin and Caden were shredding the extra class handouts to make litter for the rats that were coming to visit next week, one of them shredded the tag sheets.

They started arguing about whose fault it was. My stomach got worse as they went back and forth. I thought this might be my fault—I remembered moving some papers when I was looking for Worf. I didn't bother confessing though, since it's not really a big deal to order more stickers, and the last thing I need to do right now is add another log to my "Bertie is an idiot" fire. I kept my mouth shut and just came home.

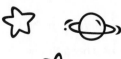

A Grave and Terrible Illness

I stayed home sick today.

My stomachache was still there this morning, so I turned down a concha at breakfast. That made it easy for Mom to say yes when I asked to stay home.

The great thing about staying home is you can watch whatever you want on TV, play video games until your eyes bleed, and eat all sorts of snacks. The bad thing about staying home when you're sick is that most of this won't appeal to you at all. I didn't even have the energy to go hunt for Izzy's hidden candy stash.

I can't sleep, and I tried watching some *Trek*, but it just didn't seem very interesting. I tried reading a pick-your-own-path book, but that didn't work either. Then I tried writing one:

Pick Your Own Path:

~~Your parents moved you to the middle of nowhere and you~~

~~Everything is your fault and you~~

That's as far as I got.

All I can think about is school.

If only I could find a big pile of butterflies to tag before the festival. Then I would win my friends back. I could be the hero Lyla mentioned.

But finding enough specimens to look amazing for the release just isn't going to happen. I looked on that forum again. There are reports everywhere that there aren't that many butterflies coming through.

I just can't go back to school and have everyone be so mad at me all the time.

There's only one thing to do: Go to a different school.

A Grave and Terrible Illness (Later)

So much for my one thing.

I tried telling Mom my big idea about switching schools. She asked me why on earth I would want to leave a school that focuses on science, and I explained about everything. And by "everything," I mean I told her everyone was mad at me for something that wasn't even my fault. She doesn't need to know more than that. If I tell her that everyone thinks Worf ate our specimens, even though I'm *pretty sure* I remembered to close her cage, she'd probably lecture me on paying attention to detail. I don't need to feel worse.

Mom sat on the end of my bed for a bit, and then she asked, "What would a Starfleet captain do? Would he leave his crew when they thought he had screwed things up, or would he try to find a way to make things work no matter how hard it is?" Then she kissed my forehead (why do moms do that?) and left.

So much for help from her.

And now I have to go back to school.

Luckily, it's Friday, so that buys me some time.

WHERE I LIVE

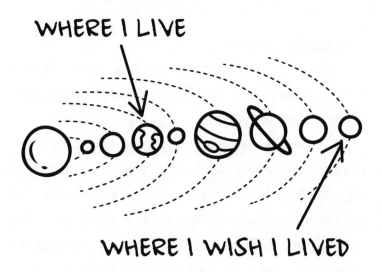

WHERE I WISH I LIVED

No Surrender

<u>Pick Your Own Path:</u>

You have lost everything and are stranded on a remote planet where the beastly inhabitants are made of ice and snow. You:

<u>A.</u> Learn all you can about the new planet and challenge everything you think you knew about it. Turn to page 15. Page 15: You think so far outside the box that you realize you aren't stranded on a planet at all, but that you are just stuck in a dream. You wake yourself up, go downstairs, and drink a bathtub full of hot cocoa.

<u>B.</u> Surrender to fate and learn to love the ice and snow and befriend the inhabitants. Turn to page 93. Page 93: You become a human icicle and develop a fear of fire. When rescue comes, you are so afraid of the rocket blasters that you hide in a cave with the beasts and are never found.

<u>C.</u> Refuse to give up. You learn everything you can about the planet in detail. Turn to page 47. Page 47: You

make a survival kit and search carefully for everything you need. You gather enough wood to light a huge fire that melts some ice beasts that try to attack you. They melt down until all that is left are normal humans who have no memory of being beasts. You end up becoming their king.

C, all the way. I refuse to give up. The clock is ticking on finding more monarchs. They usually make it to their winter roosts in the mountains of Mexico by Day of the Dead, which means they won't be migrating through here for much longer. We only have two weeks left!

I spent this afternoon rereading all the research and books I have on monarchs in detail, skipping NOTHING. Apparently, scientists find more monarchs on milkweed in planted gardens than they do on wild milkweed. But I guess it doesn't really matter, since none of us have milkweed plants in our yards. And we can't just search other people's gardens.

I also made a butterfly-catching kit to keep on me AT ALL TIMES. It includes a map of all the parks in Dallas, so in case I'm anywhere other than home, I can look and see if there's a park nearby that I can visit. My butterfly net handle was really long, so I replaced it with the telescoping handle from the broken duster downstairs. Now it fits in my backpack. I added a lidded plastic container full of glassine envelopes for transporting captured butterflies and another container for caterpillars so they don't get crushed. Then I added several plastic bags to carry milkweed plants and, of course, identification pictures of the various monarch imposters.

Meanwhile, I'm not getting anything done for Halloween or Day of the Dead! Normally, I would be working on a cool costume or decorations for the house or our ofrenda, but now I'm spending all my free time thinking about butterflies.

And you know what? I kinda like it. Don't tell Worf.

The Hidden Colony

Despite having my new kit on me all the time, I didn't catch any butterflies this morning. I think I'm seeing more though. So, this afternoon, I was in the backyard again, waiting. Dad was working in the side yard, disassembling a patio table and making a lot of noise. I sat on the back step for a while, then I did a circuit around the yard. I watched two orange-and-black butterflies fly high over my yard to the neighbor's yard. Then, finally, a third one dipped low into our yard and landed on a piece of melon I'd left on my plate from a snack. I walked over slowly and managed to net the thing before it could leave.

"Aren't you a regal monarch?" I said. "Please stay here on planet Bertie, your majesty. I guarantee you'll never have to look for flowers again." I felt someone watching me.

I slowly turned, and there was the neighbor lady, scowling over the tall fence at me. Her eyes narrowed as she saw me holding the butterfly by its wings.

"Don't you DARE rip off her wings, you little monster!" she yelled.

This surprised me, because I was expecting her to say something about crazy children talking to insects. But I'd had enough of her cranky attitude and suspicion.

I stood as tall as I could. "I'm not a monster, I'm a scientist. I'm tagging monarch butterflies to track their migration, and I would appreciate you not assuming I'm torturing them. And it's a boy—see, he has these two spots on his wings, indicating that he is, in fact, a male."

Her face softened. "That's . . . unexpected," she said. She held her breath, then let it out. "I apologize. I'm something of a butterfly person myself—in fact, I'm a retired entomologist. The kids who lived there before you weren't very nice to wildlife. When I saw your net launcher, I assumed you'd be just like them. But clearly I was wrong."

Huh. I'd just thought she was a crabby old lady. But I guess I'd misjudged her too. Maybe she could tell me where to find monarchs.

"Do you want to see him?" I asked.

She nodded, and I walked to the fence and stretched up to put the butterfly near her face. And you know what? She smiled!

"Tell me about your tagging project," she said.

I carefully slid my catch into the envelope I'd had in my pocket. I held the envelope gently in my hand (and out of the sunlight) while I explained everything about our project and how it had been hard to find specimens. I felt so comfortable talking to her that I found myself telling her about my tarantula being accused of eating our project.

"I have a pet tarantula too," she said. "And I highly doubt yours ate that many animals and left no trace. As for the lack of monarchs, well . . . would you like to search my yard?"

I checked with Dad, and he said it was okay when he saw the neighbor lady waving and nodding. I went around the gates, and when I entered her yard, I almost couldn't walk, I was so surprised.

Her yard was totally filled with flowers and plants, and there were butterflies and other insects

EVERYWHERE. I even spotted several milkweed plants with monarch caterpillars on them!

"Welcome to my insect haven. I'm Marge, by the way." She waited for a response, but I was so shocked I just stood there trying to see everything at once. "And you are Bertie," she said, chuckling. "Follow me."

I got my feet to move, and we walked through her yard to a bench by her back door and sat down.

I asked about her tarantula, and she went inside and brought out a cage that looked like it was half filled with webbing. But on one side of the cage, there was a tarantula with a brown abdomen and blue legs.

"Wow, is that a greenbottle blue tarantula?" I asked. "I can't remember the Latin name for those. Mine's a *B. hamorii.* Her name is Worf. What's your spider's name?"

"Her name is Cynthia, and yes, she's a greenbottle blue," she said. "I may study insects and not arachnids, but she was so pretty, I couldn't resist."

We talked about spiders and butterflies until I had to go home for dinner, and on the way out, she offered to let me gather any monarch butterflies or caterpillars we could find in her yard, for as long as our project goes on.

All through dinner, all I could think of was how cool Marge was. I can imagine her hanging out in her backyard covered by butterflies, like those bee guys who wear masses of live bees as beards. Only she'd be totally covered if the butterflies decided to roost together on her.

MARGE
THE BUTTERFLY LADY

After dinner, I went back to Marge's yard, and we found eight huge caterpillars and five chrysalises that the Squad could use. I was worried at first that the chrysalises might be queens, but Marge confirmed that the kind we found were monarchs. While we packed up the specimens, Marge told me that some recent research showed that monarchs in Texas roost on pecan and oak trees more frequently than other kinds of trees. And get this—the research came from a citizen science project! Citizen science really does make a difference!

Altogether, I have fourteen specimens. That's still not nearly enough to create a huge mass of butterflies for us to release at the Day of the Dead Festival, but at least I feel like I'm really helping scientists make discoveries, and I've fixed part of my mistakes since Worf "ate" thirteen specimens. Maybe it will keep some people from hating me.

The Peace Treaty

When I went to the Squad meeting today, everyone had brought in specimens. It was great to see and gave me hope for our project. I had my group from Marge's yard, and everyone else had one or two caterpillars or butterflies to add. Everyone except for Thurmond, that is. He came to the meeting late. But I'll get to that in a second.

Lyla, Caden, and Gavin were pretty impressed by my contribution. I was the only one with chrysalises, although it looked like one of Caden's caterpillars was getting close to making one, because it was huge!

I told them I was sorry that our specimens all disappeared (See how I did that? No admission of guilt, because I know Worf didn't do it!) and that I was trying really hard to get tons more. I told everyone about my kit and plans to just constantly be looking all day long until the festival came. The guys actually listened and nodded and asked questions about my kit. I

135

thought maybe they forgave me (and Worf), so I tried to negotiate a peace treaty.

"I'll bet this guy will make a chrysalis soon. Look how big and healthy he is," I said, pointing to Caden's fat caterpillar. (Peace treaty extended.)

"Yeah, I think so too," said Caden. "Um, I'm sorry I called your spider dumb, Bertie. I was just upset."

"It's okay," I said. (Peace treaty reached!)

"Yeah," said Gavin. "At least we'll have something for our booth now. Hopefully, we'll find lots more, but I haven't been having much luck. Where's Thurmond? I wonder if Captain Superior Skills has any to add?"

"You guys call him that? I thought you were his friends," said Lyla, her eyebrows raised.

"I wouldn't say we're *friends.* We're just sort of used to him," said Gavin.

Caden nodded. "He's always been sort of full of himself, but his ego is out of control this year."

"Yeah," said Gavin. "It's one of the reasons we were really wary of you, Bertie, in the beginning. We thought we'd have two Thurmonds this year."

"I hope I've convinced you I'm not that bad," I said, laughing.

"Eh, you're cool," said Gavin.

(Peace treaty fully agreed upon and signed!)

I was feeling pretty good at that point. We arranged our specimens, making sure to keep the butterflies on one end of the room and the caterpillars and chrysalises on the other to reduce chances of any contamination.

Then Thurmond arrived. He didn't have one or two specimens. He had ELEVEN butterflies.

"Check it out, you guys!" he said as he came into the lab. "I did it! I found enough to almost replace our specimens!" He looked around at us and then noticed all of our specimens on the shelves.

"Look, Bertie brought in fourteen specimens," said Lyla, waving at the shelves. "So with mine, Caden's, and Gavin's, that brings our numbers up to twenty!"

Thurmond drew his eyebrow together. "Yes, twenty. That's great." He thought for a second, then said, "But only a few are butterflies. We don't know if those chrysalises will hatch in time for the festival, so we only really have mine and those other two there to tag and release. So I still pretty much saved the day, 'cause I found a lot of butterflies, and, of course, I'll be able to find lots more."

Ugh. He couldn't handle that someone else could have found more than him. He just had to find a way to make our efforts seem less important than his!

"It'd be good to have more, but don't worry," I said. "Remember the life cycle stuff you taught us? As the animals get closer to emerging, the chrysalis changes color from green to a muted gray-black." I pointed to the chrysalises. "These are beginning to gray a bit, so these may be butterflies sooner than you think."

"The devil is in the details, Bertie. That gray could mean OE infection!" Thurmond said, crossing his arms, still trying to make our specimens seem less important.

"I don't think so," I said, smiling politely. "This coloring is symmetrical, but OE spots are asymmetrical."

"How do you even know that?"

"I've been doing a lot of detailed reading lately."

"Thurmond," said Lyla, breaking in, "aren't you happy? This means we have over thirty specimens for our project."

"Well, we'll probably lose a few to disease or something," he said. "But yeah, I'm *happy*." Still, as he said this, Thurmond stood there frowning with his arms crossed, and the tone of his voice was anything but happy.

I, on the other hand, looked like this.

The Search for Signs of Life, Day 1

We have added two butterflies that Lyla and Caden caught, and one chrysalis turned into a butterfly! It happened early this morning, so we didn't get to see it come out, but we found the butterfly in the afternoon. I wish I'd seen it. That's one more butterfly for tagging, bringing our total to sixteen. It doesn't feel like a lot, but some is better than none.

The Search for Signs of Life, Day 2

Two more chrysalises turned into butterflies! And we added one more butterfly that Lyla caught. It kind of surprises me that there are slight size differences between the individual butterflies—some really are a little smaller or bigger. I very carefully checked the smaller ones because I was worried they might be viceroys, but so far, we have all monarchs.

You know what else surprises me? Thurmond hasn't brought in any more specimens.

Too bad for him.

Time to stop writing. I've gotta go find more butterflies!

The Search for
Signs of Life, Day 3

We have two more butterflies (I found them in Marge's yard), and my last two chrysalises turned into butterflies. We also have more caterpillars turning into chrysalises. I'm starting to lose track of how many of each life stage we have, but I guess the most important thing is that we have more butterflies to tag. We've got twenty-two right now, but I still really want to have a huge swarm of butterflies to release. Demonstrating how we tag our live specimens and then releasing a whole cloud of butterflies all at once will definitely grab people's attention and get more people interested in helping!

It would be a win all around, because it might help us beat the other Squads too. I heard the seventh graders are using drones to record birdsongs, and the eighth graders are using chemistry to track water quality in our lakes here in Dallas. This means we stand a chance of beating them, because they'll have a hard time showing off that stuff at the festival. You can't drag a bunch of wild birds to your booth and convince them to sing while a drone records it, and it'd be hard to interest people in watching you test a bunch of vials of water.

Our swarm of butterflies will be more interesting than that, but we still need more! MORE!

~~The Search for Signs of Life, Day~~ Countdown to Halloween: Seven Days Away

I've been so focused on finding monarchs that I was actually surprised when I looked at the calendar the other day and realized Halloween is almost here.

Lyla came over, and we made jack-o'-lanterns today. But instead of a knife, we used a permanent marker to draw on them. I made a tarantula in a spaceship. Lyla drew a monarch butterfly holding a socket wrench.

When Lyla asked me if I wanted to trick-or-treat in her neighborhood on Halloween, I was really excited. Since we're in sixth grade now, I was worried that everyone else would think trick-or-treating was for little kids. I'm really glad that Lyla wants to go, even if she insists on wearing her handprint hat with her costume.

As far as the Squad project goes, there were no new additions today. I've been really disappointed this week that I haven't been able to find more butterflies, but Halloween is gonna be awesome. The past few days have been a blur of searching for butterflies and doing homework, so some relaxation and celebration are just what I need.

Six Days to Halloween

Twenty-three butterflies to tag. We started working on the posters for our booth at the festival today. We're making three: one explaining what our project is, one showing the life cycles of monarchs, and a special poster explaining their relationship to Day of the Dead. I hope this makes our booth look cool and gets people interested in butterfly science even though we don't have a lot of specimens.

Five Days to Halloween

Twenty-five butterflies to tag. Still not a swarm!

Four Days to Halloween

Twenty-six butterflies. We've finished making our booth backdrop and the posters. But the most important part of the booth—the specimens—still feels unfinished. Where are they all hiding? It's like they're in disguise:

I'll go look for more in a minute. But for now, I think this monarch on the left needs a cool spaceship.

Three Days to Halloween

Still twenty-six. ARGH!

Two Days to Halloween

We still just have twenty-six butterflies to release. This is depressing. It must be showing, because Izzy offered me a crusty pack of gumdrops from her candy stash. I'm almost ready to give up, but I've got to keep searching until the festival. I'm starting to wonder if the numbers of monarchs have finally dropped so low that they just don't show up in big numbers like they used to.

The Day before Halloween

Caden and Gavin brought in two butterflies today, and Lyla had two more. I added one. So at the beginning of our Squad meeting today, we were looking at thirty-one butterflies to tag at the festival.

Thurmond was late again. He arrived just as we finished practicing the last few bits of our booth presentation. And he brought a cooler that had a box inside with more monarchs folded in glassine envelopes. He had six of them, so our total jumped to thirty-seven.

I was suspicious, but I had no way to prove anything. At least these were monarchs. We were running out of shelf space and containers, so we had to decide how to store this last group.

"I have an idea!" Lyla said. "Y'all know that we can store them in coolers for transport, because they get quiescent—you know, resting like they do at night when it's dark and cold. Since we're only two days from the festival, maybe we could just leave them packed up and

Monarch butterflies spend winter in the Mexican mountains. They huddle together on trees, and some even survive snowfall. The cooler temperature causes them to become "quiescent," which is a form of inactivity or rest. If monarchs need to be transported, they can be kept folded in a closed envelope, out of the sun in a cool environment like a cooler or a refrigerator.

cooled until the morning of Day of the Dead. They'd stay nice and still in their envelopes and not get all banged up moving around a cage. Can we leave them that way for that long?"

We all searched through our notes. Except for Thurmond—he was writing in his journal, as usual. Doesn't he ever give that thing a rest?

"We can do it!" said Gavin, finally. "It says here we can store butterflies in the refrigerator in a plastic box or bag for up to two days!"

"What if they get hungry?" I asked.

"Looks like these all have had the butterfly equivalent of a big rib-feed," said Caden, inspecting the envelopes. "They all have nice fat abdomens, so they should be fine."

There wasn't really room in the lab refrigerator anymore (too much milkweed!), so we asked permission from Mr. Eagon to put them in his mini fridge out in the classroom.

When I got home this afternoon and finished my search of Marge's and our yards (no butterflies), the butterflies in the mini fridge kept coming back to me. I remembered the pictures and videos I've seen of piles and piles of monarchs in their winter roosts, covering the trunks and lower branches of the oyamel trees in the mountain forests of Mexico, just sitting there. I don't know why it stuck in my head.

Then, after dinner, I tried on my Captain Kirk costume from last year. It's too small! So I started on my backup idea to be a tarantula, but it wasn't working—the toilet-paper-tube legs looked out of proportion, and the huge mass of fine white netting I wanted to trail behind me as webbing looked stupid. It looked like I was pooping fabric.

While I was sitting there trying to decide what to do, I heard Mom downstairs saying she might make some pecan pie to put on the ofrenda for Great-Auntie Fortuna, and suddenly, it clicked: pecan trees + open water + nighttime = the best way to snag some monarchs.

I can't wait to tell Lyla about my GREAT IDEA!

But right now, I gotta do something about my costume!

Halloween
(aka THE BEST
NIGHT OF THE YEAR!)

After dinner tonight, Mom drove me over to Lyla's neighborhood because I didn't want to ride my bike in my costume—what if it came apart? Mom and Lyla's dad agreed on a later pickup time, which was great—it gave us enough time to trick-or-treat and to try out my last plan to find monarchs.

When Lyla answered the door at her house, I almost didn't recognize her. I'm so used to the coveralls and hat she usually wears that it never occurred to me she would dress in anything else for Halloween. It would make an easy costume. Instead, she was dressed as a space alien with green skin, a headband with two long antennae, a silver jacket, and a skirt on top of silver running tights. And, of course, her silver handprint hat. It was a fantastic costume.

I was speechless. She wasn't.

"What in the heck are you?" she said when she stopped laughing.

"I am a tarantula bolus," I said, waving my hands around the giant ball of netting, two-liter pop bottles cut into chunks, and torn-up toilet paper tubes. "See? A webbing ball filled with beetle parts and insect chunks?"

"I don't know if I wanna be seen with you in that getup. You look like the wrong end of a shaggy dog!"

"But . . . but," I said.

"Kidding!" she said. "That's actually really creative. Weird, but creative."

Lyla had mapped out her neighborhood, with all of the best places to go, and she brought her bike, decorated with light sticks on each spoke on the wheels. It looked pretty cool, and she added a small wagon to pull behind to carry our bags of candy as they filled up.

"Are you sure you want to tow that thing?" I asked.

"Towing is child's play when you have gear ratios," said Lyla. "And I changed this baby to a variable-speed bike this summer. Let's go!"

Some of her neighbors were giving away king-size candy bars and a small bag of candy to every kid,

except you had to go through their homemade haunted house. I hate haunted houses, but I didn't want to look like I was a chicken in front of Lyla, so I went through. I survived.

We got tons of candy, and it started to get chilly, like fall had finally decided to hit Dallas, so we went back to Lyla's, unloaded, and then went out again to search for butterflies.

When we got about eight blocks from Lyla's house, she pointed to a dimly lit cul-de-sac at the end of her development. There were new houses being built against a greenbelt, but it was mostly empty lots.

"Here it is," she said. "This area matches the description you gave me: vacant lots with pecan and oak trees, near a source of open water—there's a pond below that clearing over there. Where'd you get this idea, anyway?"

"It's perfect," I said as we walked to the first vacant lot. "I hope this works. The research Marge told me about specifically mentions monarchs roosting in pecan and oak trees in Texas. Butterflies usually roost in groups, and we already know that vacant lots and open water are good places to find them. So

I figured searching pecan and oak trees near open water at night might be the best place to find a bunch of monarchs together, and they'd be easier to catch because they are quiescent!"

"I only found one butterfly here during the day, but it's worth a shot!" said Lyla.

We searched the lots and shined our flashlights in the trees but found nothing. It took forever too. Lyla's flashlight went super dim, my feet were getting tired, and my bolus costume was getting itchy where it came up to my chin.

It was a total letdown. I really thought all that paying attention to detail would pay off. As we were walking back out of the cul-de-sac, a breeze came through and blew Lyla's antennae headband from her head. It flopped on the ground and tumbled down a barren open area between the last lot and some trees toward the pond. It stopped near a little clump of trees halfway down the hill.

"Should we go down there? There might be snakes or something," I said.

"You and your snake issue. You'd think a guy who loves spiders wouldn't be so worried about snakes."

"Nope. They're totally different. Vertebrate, invertebrate—they have nothing in common. But seriously, is it safe? I wouldn't want to risk your safety." It was a believable excuse, and it made me look like a good friend. Never mind that my greatest concern was keeping my bloodstream venom-free.

"Don't be silly," she said. "We'll go just up to the edges of those trees. See, there's no grass or anything between here and there where snakes might hide. Follow me. Just watch out for hogs."

"What?" I stopped moving.

"Boo! Kidding again!"

We arrived at the edge of the tree patch, and Lyla found her antennae. She looked closer at the trees.

"Those are pecan trees," she said.

I flicked my flashlight over the lower branches.

"Those leaves are funny looking," she said. "Did they move?"

My blood went cold. Then I thought she was kidding me again.

"Oh *yeah*," I said. "Moving bushes. Ha, ha. Happy Halloween." I moved the flashlight beam all over the trees to show her I wasn't scared, and my blood went cold again.

We'd just found a monarch roosting site full of HUNDREDS of monarch butterflies. My flashlight flickered as if it was stunned too.

"Woooow," said Lyla. "How are we going to collect them? We can't really get any closer 'cause of those tall weeds." My flashlight dimmed as she said it, and hers finally went out.

There was no way we could get the butterflies without being able to see better, and there might be snakes and/or other things in the underbrush beneath the trees. But we knew the butterflies would fly away once morning came. We needed a way to hold them there until we could come back.

"We can use my costume!" I said. I unwound the outer section of netting and spread it out on the ground. Lyla helped me pluck out the plastic bottle and cardboard pieces, and we tucked them into the netting I was still wearing so we wouldn't litter. Then we lifted the edges of the clean netting and propped it on the handles of our butterfly nets to stretch past the tall weeds toward the trees. We managed to maneuver it gently over the nearest low branch with butterflies on it. Hopefully, it will hold most of them until morning.

We returned to Lyla's house. Before Mom came and picked me up, we agreed to meet back at the lot tomorrow morning, and we'll capture as many butterflies as we can and take them to the lab at school.

I'm going to bring this journal in my bag and take it with me so I can record what happens while I'm capturing the butterflies and at the festival tomorrow.

If I'm killed by four different kinds of snakes tomorrow morning, whoever finds this journal and makes sure all the pieces of me are buried together can have my pick-your-own-path novel collection, my tarantula books, and my action figure collection, including my Ultimate Edition Mr. Spock with Mind-Meld Grip, as payment for that kindness.

Officially Signed,

Humberto Smythe-Lopez

Day of the Dead, Part 1

It's my study period, I'm alive, and I'm functioning well for not sleeping much last night.

Early this morning, before the sun came up, I left a note for Mom and Dad that I was making a last effort to get those butterflies and would see them at the festival in the afternoon. I gathered all my stuff, taped my flashlight (with fresh batteries in it) to the handlebars on my bike, and rode to meet Lyla at the butterfly site. It was cold outside, and I was super shivery. Then I remembered that's a good thing, because the butterflies wouldn't fly away until it was warm enough. So I sucked it up and didn't complain.

When I arrived, we set up some camping lamps that Lyla brought in her bike wagon. We had to work fast to make sure we got the butterflies before the sun came up and warmed them. But since they were cold and still, they were so much easier to collect than during the day. We packed as many specimens as we could get in envelopes and placed the envelopes in groups in small cardboard boxes. Then we stacked the boxes in a cooler lined with cold packs to keep the butterflies safe and still while they were being transported.

I was dead tired by the time we got to school, even though Lyla's bike was dragging the wagon with the butterfly cooler and lamps in it. I guess gear ratios and having variable speeds really help, because she looked wide awake and was barely out of breath at all.

We got to school early, but the teachers were already there. Mr. Eagon was completely amazed by our discovery. We decided to leave the cooler on the floor of the lab until this afternoon when we do setup.

Then I had this great idea to share my technique for finding the roost with the people in that butterfly forum and invite them all to come and see the butterflies at our festival.

Lyla came with me to the computer lab. I was flipping past all the posts from my previous searches (including a bunch by that guy CowboyFan) that I'd saved to my profile when I noticed a saying in the signature line of CowboyFan's posts: "The devil is in the details."

Thurmond's favorite quote!

I showed it to Lyla and told her about CowboyFan. Then we looked up his user profile.

"He's listed as being in Dallas," Lyla said, reading the screen. "And a 'cowboy fan' around here is a fan of the Dallas Cowboys football team. Football is Thurmond's favorite sport, but there could be other Cowboys fans living in Dallas who want to find butterflies."

"But how many of them would use that quote?" I asked. "CowboyFan HAS to be Thurmond."

"Maybe, but how can we prove it?" Lyla asked. "His name isn't anywhere. Even if it were, it doesn't prove he cheated, since there aren't any posts showing that he actually bought anything from the butterfly farm."

Neither of us had an answer, and now it's driving me crazy.

How are we going to catch him?

Day of the Dead, Part 2

Wow. Just WOW. The festival was CRAZY! Where to start?

We began setup this afternoon during sixth period. Caden and Gavin arrived in the lab, and Lyla and I astounded them with our mass of butterflies and our new technique. Then we told them about our CowboyFan theory.

"You know what? We can't prove anything," said Caden, "and we have a ton of work to do for the festival. Let's just focus on that for now. Mr. Eagon is already waiting for us at the booth."

"He's right," said Gavin. "I wanna see Thurmond get caught, but right now, we've gotta focus on this hailstorm of butterflies you brought in. How are we going to tag them all before the planned release time? We can't change the time, because it's already printed on the schedule."

"What if instead of just demonstrating how we tag the butterflies, we actually teach people how to do the tagging themselves at the booth during the presentation?" said Lyla. "I can add that into my part of the presentation about how to tag, and then we can invite people to stick around and help. Anyone else who wanders up to our booth after the presentation can help too. Then a whole bunch of people get to be citizen scientists!"

That solved it. We got to work gathering our stuff to take out to the festival booth area in the courtyard, then Gavin and Caden started moving those things while Lyla and I did the daily feeding and cleaning of our remaining caterpillars. I tried not to think about CowboyFan.

Then Thurmond showed up with *another* box of monarchs.

"Behold your hero," he said, trying to make it sound like he was joking. "Look at what I caught yesterday: FORTY butterflies! I'm a butterfly genius! This is the part where you're impressed because I saved the day!"

"Wait, what?" said Gavin suspiciously. "You caught these all on Halloween too? What's your technique?"

"No technique, just superior searching skills. Wait—what do you mean 'too'?" said Thurmond, frowning.

"Lyla and Bertie found a roost last night and got a whole bunch of specimens this morning. Look!" said Caden, opening the cooler we brought.

"Well," said Thurmond, eyes narrow, "we once again have lots of specimens for our project. This is . . . great." He said it with no enthusiasm.

I watched Gavin and Caden leave the classroom with our booth display materials, and I noticed Thurmond's journal on the counter in the back of the class—and it was open. He was always writing something in there. What if he wrote something about how he got the butterflies? I had to get a look in it. Lyla saw what I was looking at and nodded. She took off her gloves, washed her hands, and grabbed the next big box of butterfly containers to go to the booth.

"Hey, can you help me carry this box?" she said really loud. "I want to make sure the box is steady, so the butterflies don't get too banged-up, but it's too heavy." I knew exactly what she was doing. If she could get him out of the room, I could read his journal.

Thurmond fell for it. "I'll help you, Lyla. I've got steady hands," he said.

They left, and I ran into the classroom and flipped open his journal. It was ALL there in detail: his username, his records—everything! And it was WAY worse than I thought.

Thurmond bought queen caterpillars from the butterfly farm because that was all they had available, and he figured no one would know the difference at the caterpillar stage. Then he'd FAKED the specimens dying off so we wouldn't catch him when we learned there are monarch look-alikes! He snuck in really early in the morning through the window in the lab with the loose latch and took the specimens home with him and raised them, including MY caterpillar, which was a monarch!

AND HE FRAMED WORF! He stole the next batch of specimens too and opened the lid of Worf's cage to make it look like she did it!

Then he BOUGHT these last two batches of monarchs as the farmer had them available.

My rush of excitement that I'd finally caught him was quickly replaced by panic as I realized he was about to let us tag and release commercially raised monarchs

169

into the wild population, which could be a total disaster for those wild ones. We were about to launch nearly FIFTY flying butterfly bombs!

Pick Your Own Path:

Today you must make a decision that may impact your life forever. A teammate in the Quest for Knowledge Game is cheating. Having more ~~monarch specimens to tag~~ material and resources in The Game will make your group more competitive in the eyes of The Gamemakers, but uncovering the truth may hurt your team by losing a member of an already tiny ragtag group and possibly ruin your only chance to ~~beat out the other Squads and~~ go to the next level in the Quest for Knowledge Game. You:

_A_. Do something stupid.

_B_. Do something selfish.

_C_. Decide the truth must be known because it is the right thing to do. You move forward to reveal the teammate's actions, whatever the cost.

Of course, I picked C. I didn't really see any other choice. I checked the lab for Thurmond's specimens, but they were already down at the booth. I grabbed his journal and sprinted to the courtyard.

As I opened the doors to the courtyard, I felt like I'd walked into a nightmare. The air was warm and sunny now as the sun rotated over the school, making me feel too hot in my long-sleeve shirt. But what really got me was that the air was full of orange-and-black butterflies—which meant our monarchs must have escaped from the cages while I was inside.

Of course, this would happen just when I was finally accepted by the Squad! It was probably going to be my fault again, and I would never be able to cope at school. Maybe I could convince Mom to move us all the way to Mexico.

The butterflies flitted around me as I ran to the booth.

"What happened?" I asked Lyla, waving my hand at the loose butterflies surrounding us. "How'd our cages get open?"

"They didn't," she said. On the table behind her, the monarch cages were still full, our collected butterflies safely inside. "All of those in the air are wild ones!"

Looking up, it was like someone had draped strings of butterflies across the courtyard like party lights. And more seemed to be coming! The nightmare was actually a dream come true! Swarms of wild monarchs! I suddenly remembered why I'd come out here so fast.

Thurmond was in the booth, trying to open the lid of his Big Box o' Butterfly Bombs.

"Don't do it!" I yelled.

The Squad all stopped what they were doing.

Thurmond rolled his eyes. "I have to unpack them if we're going to tag them."

"Are you sure about that, CowboyFan?"

"What?"

"You left your journal open in the lab." I held up the journal.

Thurmond turned sheet-white. Then he put the box of butterflies on the table and snatched the journal from me. "That's mine!"

I grabbed the box of monarchs, but he tried to grab them too.

"You can't let these go in the wild, and you KNOW it!" I yelled, pulling harder.

Mr. Eagon had been talking to another teacher nearby, but he came over to us, his eyes locked on the box and the journal. "What's going on, boys?"

I wrestled with wanting to yell to everyone in the courtyard that Thurmond was a cheater. I felt the words forming, but I looked at the faces of the rest of the Squad and our amazing booth. I imagined us getting to represent the school at the city competition. I didn't need to embarrass the whole Squad. I swallowed the words.

"Ask Thurmond," I said instead, letting go of the box.

Mr. Eagon turned to face Thurmond. "Is there something you want to tell me, Thurmond?"

"I . . . I," said Thurmond nervously.

From behind Mr. Eagon, I glared at Thurmond and pointed to the journal. I could see the panic in his eyes. There was no way out for him. That journal laid it all out in his own handwriting. If he didn't say it, the journal would.

"These monarchs are . . . they're, uh . . ." He closed his eyes. "They're commercially raised." He hung his head.

The Squad all gasped, and Mr. Eagon frowned, then cleared his throat. "Then we need to separate them from the project specimens. Let's carry them to the office, and you can tell me more about why they are here." Then he quickly gathered all of Thurmond's specimens and motioned for Thurmond to come with him.

Once again, the Squad was a bunch of silent glares. But this time, their anger was directed at Thurmond.

"I just wanted us to have a lot of butterflies and win everything: the badges, the chance at the city competition, the—what'd you call it, Lyla?—adoration," Thurmond babbled in a low voice, looking at Lyla as Mr. Eagon tried to escort him away. "But finding specimens was just so HARD! And then Lyla said . . . Well, I just wanted to be the hero, but no matter what I did, all she noticed was Bertie! It's not right! I have the highest IQ, the most stickers, and I was the one willing to put everything on the line . . ." his voice faded as they walked away.

The rest of the Squad came and gathered by me. Lyla looked like she was gonna barf. I patted her arm awkwardly.

"That was category five!" said Gavin.

"Oh my God, we're all going to get in trouble," said Caden. "They'll think we were all cheating!"

"I don't think so," I said. "It's all in that journal. He recorded it all in detail: how many specimens he bought, when he bought them, how many he had compared to all of us. He even made fun of us for 'doing it the old-fashioned way.'"

"Oh man, that is SO wrong," said Gavin.

I nodded in agreement. "What he did may be wrong, but he was right about one thing."

"What could that *possibly* be?" asked Lyla, scowling.

"The devil IS in the details," I replied.

Day of the Dead, Part 3

Whoops, had a hand cramp. It's better now. Maybe I shouldn't hold my pencil so hard when I write—I snapped the tip twice when I wrote that last page.

Anyway, long story short, we finished setting up our booth. Mr. Eagon eventually came back and said the judges talked and that it was okay to go ahead and present, and that we were cleared of suspicion. He said we would need to proceed without Thurmond—if we still wanted to try. Of course we did!

Marge showed up a few minutes later, along with my family and some more wild monarchs for us to tag. I asked her about all of the butterflies flying overhead.

"It's been a late migration this year—that happens sometimes," she said. "I noticed the numbers were low the past two months, and then, suddenly, just in the past few days, they spiked." She said it was because the weather was warmer this fall, and that confused the butterflies.

When the crowd gathered to see our presentation, we were all a little nervous, especially since I had to fill in Thurmond's part about the life cycle. But it felt really good that the other Squad members picked me to do it. When we got to Lyla's part about how to catch and tag the butterflies, she was able to actually catch one of the wild ones right then and there in front of everyone!

People really liked helping to tag the butterflies. And it's a good thing we had that help too, since Thurmond never came back. I know I'm not the only one who wonders whether Thurmond will be expelled or just suspended for this.

Lyla was right: My fingers were the best at getting those stickers on the butterflies. At least they *were*, until Izzy and her fingers tried. She was REALLY good at placing tags, and very patient. Marge said Izzy could help with the butterflies in Marge's backyard, and Izzy looked like someone had just given her the keys to the candy store. Maybe little sisters have some use after all.

As butterflies were tagged, we recorded the data for each one's tag number, and then we placed the specimens in the giant mesh cages we'd brought to hold them for the release. They looked like big pop-up laundry hampers full of butterflies.

I think our booth was the most popular booth at the festival—or at least of the portion that was in the courtyard. Somehow, I missed the fact that this festival included a carnival and rides outside in the parking lot. You would think that I would have noticed it on the posters, but I guess I was so absorbed in butterflies that I completely missed it.

Anyway, I wonder if the swarms of migrating butterflies were attracted to our area because the courtyard was decorated with bright, multicolored tissue-paper banners, and the booths were all decorated in similar festive colors. The courtyard looked like it could be a giant space garden full of mutant flowers.

It was cool to see all the different aspects of Day of the Dead interpreted in so many different ways at all those colorful booths. The cooking club was selling spiced hot chocolate and fresh-from-the-oven pastries and breads. The dance team was preparing for an interpretive dance celebrating the lives of departed family members. Art classes each had different booths

showing their art or crafts for Day of the Dead
celebrations.

Even the other Science Squad booths were pretty
impressive. The seventh graders added colored lights
to their drones as they flew them around for their
demonstration, and Barton Twisp and the other eighth
graders used colored paper and flashing lights to
decorate the posters explaining their water testing.
Still, I'm pretty sure we're going to be the team
representing Brenton Park at the city-level Science
Squad competition.

When we took breaks and explored, I had the best
time. It's so awesome having a group of friends. The
first break, Caden and I went straight to the cooking
club booth and gulped down hot chocolate and ate some
pan de muerto covered in pink sugar. Then we got sugar
skulls and decorated them and gnawed their crispness
until our teeth hurt.

I went on break later with Lyla and Gavin. We
walked among the tables that had examples of Day of
the Dead altars set up by families to honor their loved
ones, and we talked about the idea that the butterflies
were the souls of people going home to Mexico to visit

their families. Butterflies were drawn to the tables because they had offerings of the deceased's favorite foods, and some were cut fruits. Watching butterflies eat fruit is so much more interesting when you think of them as souls fueling up to head home for a visit.

Then Gavin went in the hurricane simulator, which we now call the hurl-a-cane barf-a-lator!

When we got back to the booth, the last few monarchs were tagged and recorded. A huge crowd gathered to watch the release. We unzipped the cages, and the butterflies climbed out and joined the wild ones flying overhead. It wasn't a tornado, but it was a LOT, and it was AWESOME! Everywhere, black-and-orange royalty lifted their wings and joined the crowd for the long journey back to their great-grandparents' birthplaces.

"You know," I said, looking up, "I wish that we could do monarch research next year in seventh grade."

"That would be great," said Lyla. "We could follow individual butterflies with the drones along part of their migration route or something. Or maybe we could use them to find butterfly roosteries. I don't care what, just as long as we don't use them in food fights!"

As they fluttered around us and flew away, I thought about how most of those butterflies were probably born somewhere else, but they managed to find milkweed and flowers and other butterflies wherever they went. I may be living miles from where I grew up, but I found a lot of awesome things here in Dallas, even friends.

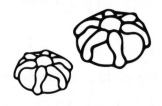

A New Beginning

Congratulations, space cadet! Your mission to find new life on other planets has been a success!

You survived basic training, learned about a new species, found the king, turned neighboring enemies into friends, vanquished the traitor in your ranks, and survived terrible losses in this new place that you now call home. You've found green on the barren planet, and the lizard people have all turned out to be normal people wearing hats. Best of all, you have yet to encounter any ~~venomous snakes~~ giant meteor-size space serpents.

The peace treaty with your new allies has worked out very well. In fact, you've been so busy hanging out with all your ~~friends~~ allies that you forgot to do your captain's log for several weeks. Here's what's happened:

A. You've had your first story published in ~~the school magazine~~ a magazine for star explorers. Of course, it was a pick-your-own-path story, and the fans have been begging for more. (Ms. Finch wants three more to publish this year!)

B. Your team's efforts were so inspiring that several people have signed up to join the ranks of the star explorers, and you received awards for it! (The Monarch Tag and Track people said they had a jump in sign-ups for next year's tagging project and that several of those people specifically listed the Brenton Park team as the referral source! We all got stickers for research AND education!!)

C. The Gamemakers decided that your team will represent ~~Brenton Park~~ the Science Academy at the ~~citywide Science Squad competition~~ Brain Games Expo on Orion 5! (We beat the seventh and eighth graders!!!!! Thurmond would have been impressed. Too bad he lost his spot at Brenton Park and had to switch schools!)

You picked your path, but this adventure ends here. The only question left is this:

What are you going to do next?

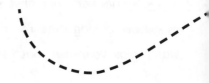

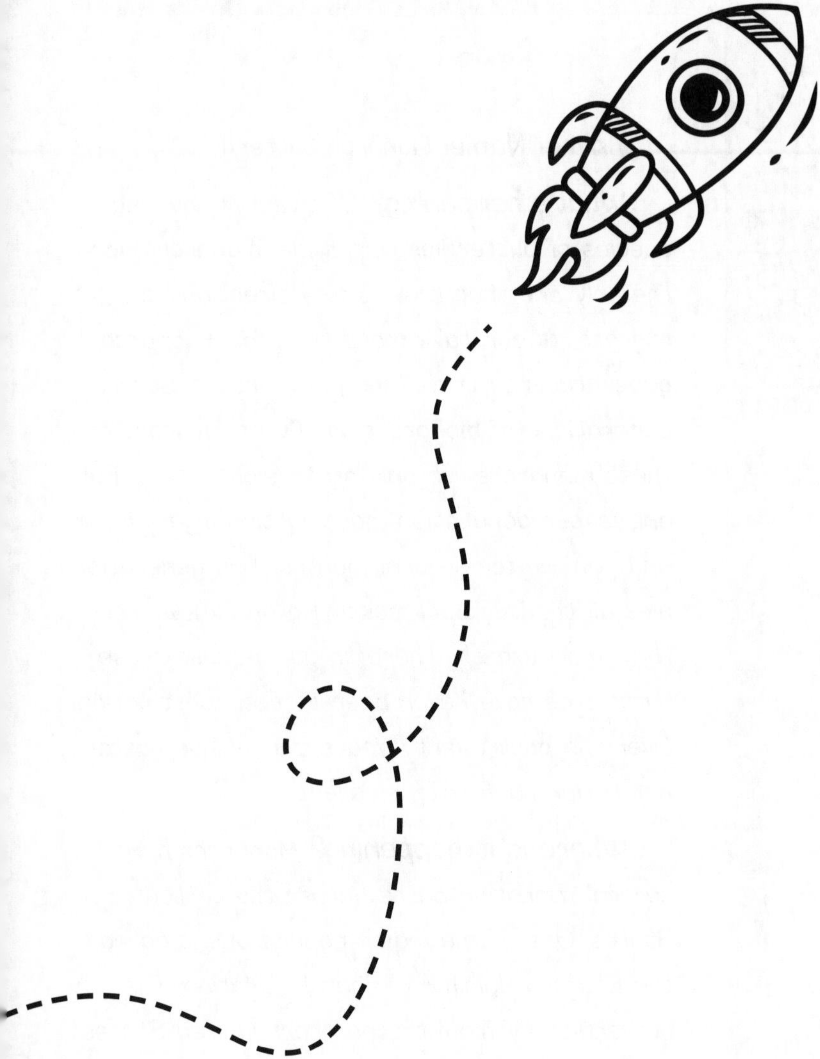

Animal Name: Monarch butterfly

What's happening? Of twenty thousand species of butterflies worldwide, monarchs are the only one that travels two directions to migrate. It can take more than four monarch generations to travel the entire route. Several generations of monarchs will fly north. Most of these monarchs live only six to eight weeks. But one "super generation" has slightly larger wings and can live for several months. This generation flies all the way back south. No one knows how they know exactly where to go, because these butterflies have never been to their destination. Over the past twenty years, this unique butterfly population has grown smaller.

Where is it happening? Monarchs have several migration paths across the United States. One of the major populations is called the Eastern North American Population. These butterflies fly from the northern United States and Canada to Mexico in the fall. After wintering in Mexico, they start heading north again in the spring.

Why is it important? If monarchs disappear, we will never know why they are unique. In addition, monarchs are important pollinators. Without them, many plants will be unable to grow. Some of these plants, such as alfalfa and red clover, are food for animals. Others, such as apple trees, provide food for humans.

In the Field

Dr. Karen Oberhauser has studied monarch butterflies for more than thirty years. She has researched many issues that affect monarchs, ranging from parasites to milkweed loss to climate change, and the impact of these issues on migration. She is currently the director of the University of Wisconsin-Madison Arboretum.

One of her greatest contributions to scientific research though, is supporting citizen science, where scientists partner with everyday people to gather scientific data. In 2013, Oberhauser was recognized with the White House Citizen Science Champion of Change Award for her efforts creating monarch citizen science programs.

The number of monarchs has dropped in recent years, but Oberhauser believes citizen science brings hope for conservation. The amount of data collected by citizen science programs allows scientists to make discoveries that would be, as Oberhauser says, "completely impossible if scientists were just going out and collecting data on their own." These programs could help scientists finally unlock the mysteries of monarch migration.

Glossary

chrysalis – The third stage in a butterfly's four-part life cycle. A chrysalis can also be called a pupa.

entomologist – A scientist who studies insects.

flyway – The route or path that a group of migrating animals uses regularly for migration.

frass – The waste of the larval stage of an insect.

larva – The second stage in an insect's four-part life cycle. Butterfly larvae are often called caterpillars.

migration – The mass movement of animals from one place to another, usually done in specific seasons over a long distance.

parasite – A living thing that uses another living thing for survival in a one-sided relationship that is only good for the parasite.

pollinator – An animal that carries pollen from plant to plant, which helps the plants to grow.

proboscis – A long, thin body part that butterflies use to sip food.

protozoan – A tiny, single-celled animal.

protuberance – A part that sticks out from something else. Monarch caterpillars have two pairs of protuberances, one set of which are antennae.

Selected Bibliography

"Migration & Tagging." *Monarch Watch*,
    www.monarchwatch.org/tagmig/tag.htm.
    Accessed November 10, 2017.

"Monarch Butterflies." *Journey North*,
    www.learner.org/jnorth/monarchs. Accessed
    November 10, 2017.

"Monarch Butterfly: What is Citizen Science?"
    *United States Department of Agriculture
    Forest Service*, www.fs.fed.us/wildflowers/
    pollinators/Monarch_Butterfly/citizenscience/
    index.shtml. Accessed November 10, 2017.

"Study Monarchs: Citizen Science Opportunities."
    Monarch Joint Venture, monarchjointventure.
    org/getinvolved/study-monarchs-citizen-
    scienceopportunities. Accessed November 10,
    2017.

About the Author

Amanda Humann lives in Seattle, Washington, where she writes and draws stuff for a living. When she isn't doing those things, she enjoys games, puzzles, cooking, ~~studying weird plants and animals, asking questions, and blowing stuff up~~ science, and eating candy. Her honors for writing include the American Library Association Young Adult Library Services Association's 2014 Quick Picks for Reluctant Young Adult Readers.

About the Illustrator

Arpad Olbey is an illustrator veteran and art director of his art studio in London. He works with paper, pencils, and paints, or digital high-tech equipment, depending on the project. His wish is to combine his experience and technical knowledge to deliver the best that his creativity can give to audiences.

Explore Even More
SCIENCE SQUAD!

by J. A. Watson   Illustrated by Arpad Olbey

AVAILABLE NOW!